Elmet

Elmet

FIONA MOZLEY

HarperCollins*Publishers*Ltd

Published by HarperCollins Publishers Ltd,
by arrangement with Algonquin Books of Chapel Hill,
a division of Workman Publishing Company, Inc., New York.

Originally published in the United Kingdom in 2017 by JM Originals,
an imprint of John Murray (Publishers), an Hachette UK Company.
First published in Canada in 2017 by HarperCollins Publishers Ltd
in this original trade paperback edition.

HarperCollins books may be purchased for educational, business,
or sales promotional use through our Special Markets Department.

HarperCollins Publishers Ltd
2 Bloor Street East, 20th Floor
Toronto, Ontario, Canada
M4W 1A8

www.harpercollins.ca

Library and Archives Canada Cataloguing in Publication
information is available upon request.

ISBN 978-1-44345-603-6

Printed and bound in the United States
LSC/H 9 8 7 6 5 4 3 2

For Megan

'Elmet was the last independent Celtic kingdom in England and originally stretched out over the vale of York . . . But even into the seventeenth century this narrow cleft and its side-gunnels, under the glaciated moors, were still a 'badlands', a sanctuary for refugees from the law'

Remains of Elmet
Ted Hughes

I

I cast no shadow. Smoke rests behind me and daylight is stifled. I count sleepers and the numbers rush. I count rivets and bolts. I walk north. My first two steps are slow, languid. I am unsure of the direction but in that initial choice I am pinned. I have passed through the turnstile and the gate is locked.

I still smell embers. The charred outline of a sinuous wreck. I hear those voices again: the men, and the girl. The rage. The fear. The resolve. Then those ruinous vibrations coursing through wood. And the lick of the flames. The hot, dry spit. The sister with blood on her skin and that land put to waste.

I keep to the railway tracks. I hear an engine far off in the distance and duck behind a hawthorn. There are no passengers; only freight. Steel wagons emblazoned with rogue emblems: the heraldry of youth long grown old. Rust and grit and decades of smog.

Rain comes then stops. The weeds are drenched. The soles of my shoes squeak against the grasses. If my muscles begin to ache I do not reckon with them. I run. I walk. I run some more. I drag my feet. I rest. I drink from alcoves into which the rainwater has pooled. I rise. I walk.

There is always doubt. If she turned south when she came to the railway there is no use. She will never be found. I can walk or I can jog or I can sprint or I can just stop in the middle of the tracks and lie down and wait for a train to cut through me; it would make no odds. If she turned south she is lost.

But I chose the way north so that is the way I will go.

I break all bonds. I step through the margins of fields. I scale barbed-wire fences and locked gates. I cut through industrial estates and private gardens. I pay no mind to the lines of counties and boroughs and parishes. I walk, whether paddock or pasture or park.

The tracks take me between hills. The trains glide below peaks with dales underneath. I spend an evening laid out on a moor, watching the wind, the crows, the distant vehicles; caught in memories of this same land, further south; earlier, another time; then likewise caught in memories of home, of family, of the shifts and turns in fortune, of beginnings and endings, of causes and consequences.

The next morning I continue on my way. The remains of Elmet lie beneath my feet.

Chapter One

We arrived in summer when the landscape was in full bloom and the days were long and hot and the light was soft. I roamed shirtless and sweated cleanly and enjoyed the hug of the thick air. In those months I picked up freckles on my bony shoulders and the sun set slowly and the evenings were pewter before they were black, before the mornings seeped through again. Rabbits gambolled in the fields and when we were lucky, when the wind was still and a veil settled on the hills, we saw a hare.

Farmers shot vermin and we trapped rabbits for food. But not the hare. Not my hare. A dam, she lived with her drove in a nest in the shadow of the tracks. She was hardened to the passing of the trains and when I saw her I saw her alone as if she had crept out of the nest unseen and unheard. It was a rare thing for creatures of her kind to leave their young in summer and run through the fields. She was searching. Searching for food or for a mate. She searched as if she were a hunting animal, as if she were a hare who had thought again and decided not to be prey but rather to run and to hunt, as if she were a hare who found herself chased one day by a fox and stopped suddenly and turned and chased back.

Whatever the reason, she was unlike any other. When she darted I could barely see her but when she stopped for a moment she was the stillest thing for miles around. Stiller than the oaks and pines. Stiller even than the rocks and pylons. Stiller than the railway tracks. It was as if she had grabbed hold of the earth and pinned it down with her at its centre, and even the quietest, most benign landmarks spun outrageously around, while all of it, the whole scene, was suckered in by her exaggerated, globular, amber eye.

And if the hare was made of myths then so too was the land at which she scratched. Now pocked with clutches of trees, once the whole county had been woodland and the ghosts of the ancient forest could be marked when the wind blew. The soil was alive with ruptured stories that cascaded and rotted then found form once more and pushed up through the undergrowth and back into our lives. Tales of green men peering from thickets with foliate faces and legs of gnarled timber. The calls of half-starved hounds rushing and panting as they snatched at charging quarry. Robyn Hode and his pack of scrawny vagrants, whistling and wrestling and feasting as freely as the birds whose plumes they stole. An ancient forest ran in a grand strip from north to south. Boars and bears and wolves. Does, harts, stags. Miles of underground fungi. Snowdrops, bluebells, primroses. The trees had long since given way to crops and pasture and roads and houses and railway tracks and little copses, like ours, were all that was left.

Daddy and Cathy and I lived in a small house that Daddy built with materials from the land here about. He chose for us a small ash copse two fields from the east coast main line, far enough not to be seen, close enough to know the trains well. We heard them often enough: the hum and ring of the passenger trains, the choke and gulp of the freight, passing by with their cargo tucked behind in painted metal tanks. They had timetables and intervals of their own, drawing growth rings around our house with each journey, ringing past us like prayer chimes. The long, indigo Adelantes and Pendolinos that streaked from London to Edinburgh. The smaller trains that bore more years, with rust on their rattling

pantographs. Old carthorse-trains chugging up to
the knacker, they moved too slowly for the younger
tracks and slipped on the hot-rolled steel like old
men on ice.

On the day we arrived an old squaddy drove up the
hill in an articulated lorry filled with cracked and
discarded stone from an abandoned builders' yard.
The squaddy let Daddy do most of the unloading
while he sat on a freshly cut log and smoked cigarette
after cigarette that Cathy rolled from her own tobacco
and papers. He watched her closely as she spun them
with her fingers and tipped tongue over teeth to lick
the seal. He looked at her right thigh as she rested
the tobacco pouch upon it and more than once leaned
over to pick it up, brushing his hand against her as
he did so, then pretending to read the text on the
packet. He offered to light her cigarettes for her each
time. He held out the flame eagerly and took offence,
like a child, when she continued to light them herself.
He could not see that she was scowling the whole
time and frowning at her hands as she did his work.
He was not a man who could look and see and understand faces well enough to tell. He was not one of
those who know what eyes and lips mean or who can
imagine that a pretty face might not be closed around
pretty thoughts.

7

The squaddy talked all afternoon about the army and the fighting he had done in Iraq and in Bosnia and how he had seen boys as young as me slashed open with knives, their innards a passing blue. There was little darkness in him when he told us this. Daddy worked on the house during the day and in the evening the two grown men went down the hill to drink some of the cider the squaddy had brought in a plastic pop bottle. Daddy did not stay long. He did not like drinking much and he did not like company save for me and my sister.

When Daddy came back he told us that he had an argument with the squaddy. He had clouted the squaddy about the head with his left fist and now had a bloody nick in his skin just by the thumb knuckle.

I asked him what had started the argument.

'He were a bastard, Daniel,' Daddy said to me. 'He were a bastard.'

Cathy and I thought that was fair enough.

Our house was laid out like any bungalow or park home on the outskirts of any smallish city where old people and poor families live. Daddy was no architect but he could follow a grey and white schematic rustled from the local council offices.

Our house was stronger than others of its type

though. It was built with better bricks, better mortar, better stones and timber. I knew it would last many dozen seasons longer than those houses we saw on the roads into town. And it was more beautiful. The green mosses and ivies from the wood were more eager to grip at its sides, more ready to pull it back into the landscape. Every season the house looked older than it was and the longer it looked to have been there the longer we knew it would last. Like all real houses and all those that call them home.

As soon as the external walls were up I planted seeds and bulbs. The earth was still open from the foundations Daddy dug. I extended the troughs and filled them with compost and fresh manure we got from a stable eight miles down the way where little girls in fawn jodhpurs and shining leather boots rode ponies around a floodlit gymkhana. I planted pansies and daffodils and roses of all different colours and a cutting taken from a white-flowering climbing plant I found spewing out of an old drystone wall. It was the wrong time of year to plant but some shoots came up and more came the following year. Waiting is what a true house is about. Making it ours, making it settle, pinning it and us to the seasons, to the months and to the years.

We came there soon before my fourteenth birthday when Cathy had just turned fifteen. It was early summer, which gave Daddy the time to build. He knew we would be finished well before winter and there was enough of a structure to live in by the middle of September. Before then we made our home from two decommissioned army vans that Daddy had bought from a thief in Doncaster and driven to the site down back roads and tracks. We hooked them together with steel rope and tarpaulin was stretched over the top, expertly and securely, to give us shelter beneath. Daddy slept in one van and Cathy and I in the other. Under the tarpaulin there were weathered, plastic garden chairs and after some time a sunken blue sofa. We used that as our living room. We used upturned boxes to rest our mugs and plates above the ground and to rest our feet too, on warm summer evenings when there was nothing to do but sit and talk and sing.

On the clearest evenings we stayed out until morning. We clicked on the radios from both vans and Cathy and I danced on the leafy earth to our woodland stereo, safe in the knowledge any neighbour was too far to hear. Sometimes we sat and sang without the radios. Years ago, Daddy had bought me a wooden recorder and Cathy a violin. We had had free lessons when we were still at school. We were not experts but made a decent sound because of the instruments we played. Daddy had chosen well. He knew nothing of music but a great deal about fine objects. He could pick out craft and quality by the woods and the glues and the smell of the varnish and the smoothness of the edges. We had driven all the way to Leeds for them.

He knew about different woods, you see. He got to know the trees that lived in our copse early on and showed them to me. Almost all were between saplings and fifty years old as the copse had been coppiced well since long before we had moved there, for hundreds of years, even, Daddy thought. In the centre, right at the heart, there were older trees and one was the oldest of them all. The mother, Daddy said, from which all the others had come. She had been there for over two hundred years and her bark was set hard like scraped kauri gum.

There were hazel trees too and some of those dropped nuts. Daddy cut branches away from the trunks and showed me how to work the greenwood with a sharp folding knife. I spent days trying to fashion a thin flute from fresh greenwood, whittling the soft bark away from the sinew and gouging out the fleshy innards. I worked precisely to make the outside as smooth as I could, curved like a finger. But the flute did not sound and after that I moved towards making things that were useful, objects that required less skill, or rather, things that were able to exist even if they were not precisely so. As long as a bowl holds its charge it is easy to define even if it is ugly and rough. But if a flute does not make a musical note it cannot be called a flute.

Our home in the woods had a kitchen and a large oak table. When we still camped, Daddy cooked on a barbecue he had made from pieces of corrugated iron and charcoal that he had baked in two oil drums in the heart of the copse near the old mother tree.

We ate too much meat in those days. We followed Daddy's diet so ate the food he had cooked for himself before we had come to live with him permanently. This was mainly the meat he hunted. He did not care for fruit or vegetables. He hunted wood pigeon, rock dove, collared dove, pheasant and woodcock, if he caught them in the evenings coming out of cover. There were muntjac around too and when there was too little to hunt or when he had cash in his pocket or when he just fancied a change he went into the village and bargained for joints of beef, lamb or pork sausages. In the right season there was smaller game for breakfast. A man in the village had a merlin and with it he caught too many skylarks to eat alone so gave them to us in exchange for birds that were too big for the merlin to steal. We ate the skylarks on toast, almost whole, with mugs of hot, milky tea.

Once Daddy went away with the travellers for four days and returned with a hessian sack of plucked ducks and five crates of live chickens. He constructed a coop for the chickens near where the back door of the house was going to be. We ate eggs after that but still hardly any vegetables or fruit except berries from the sides of the roads.

It was later, when the house was built, that I planted apple and plum trees and asked Daddy to bring sacks of carrots and parsnips from the village when he went down there for business. I prepared what he brought on the scrubbed kitchen table with knives my Daddy had sharpened.

Before the house was built, in those few hot, dry months when we camped and sang, Daddy talked to us properly. He used few words but we heard much more. He spoke of the men he had fought and the men he had killed, in the peat fields of Ireland or that black mud of Lincolnshire that clings to the hands and feet like forensic ink. Daddy boxed for money with bare knuckles far from gymnasiums or auditoriums but the money could be big and men whose cash came from nowhere arrived from across the country to lay their bets on him to win. Anyone was a fool not to back my Daddy. He could knock a man out with just one punch and if it lasted longer it was because he wanted a full fight.

The bouts were arranged by travellers or rough men from around who desired the chance to test themselves and earn a slice of cash. The travellers had fought in this way for centuries. 'Prize Fights' or 'Fair Fights' they called them. They wore no padded gloves nor did they divide the bouts into rounds with breaks. These men would not fight for the splitting peace-toll of the bell but until one surrendered or was bludgeoned cold. Sometimes the fights rested disputes between warring clans. As often as not they were for money. Tens of thousands of pounds could be settled and Daddy made a decent living from it.

There was a feud that had run for decades, Daddy told us, between the Joyces and the Quinn-McDonaghs. Every three years or so they would send their young men out against each other in one-on-one bare-knuckle matches that were moderated by older men from neutral families. In cases like these the families themselves could not be present in case a brawl broke out between one clan and the other, old and young, men and women, and a whole portion of the travelling community was wiped out or arrested by the police and packed into vans and taken off to jail.

There was much to gain. These feud fights were not divorced from high stakes. The Joyces and Quinn-McDonaghs competed on how much cash they were willing to front. Sometimes as much as £50,000 each and the winner would take it all back to their caravan and treat the whole clan to an evening of whisky. Daddy said they wanted the fights. He said that after all this time the quarrel between the families meant little but each time one of the top men was short of money they would like as not start something up in the hope of gaining. It was more than pride; it was prize money.

This is what it was about for Daddy too, of course. We were not travellers so the feuds meant nothing to us. He fought at bouts that were arranged for money, where travellers or gypsies, rough farmers, criminals from the towns, owners of underground nightclubs and bars, drug dealers and thugs, or just men who saw their worth resting in their fists, met together and brought their money in the hope of winning more. Daddy arrived in a pair of blue jeans and a buttoned-up bomber jacket. He was given the time and place over the phone by a fixer or else just picked up by the travellers or by someone else. He waited quietly among his admirers. Daddy rarely talked more than he could help. He allowed very few men to meet his eyes. He turned away and paced calmly by himself while the men made their bargains and agreed their rates.

Daddy started the fight. He peeled off his jacket and jumper and stood in a white vest, revealing not the lean, stratiform muscles of an athlete but the kind of biceps that could be soft tight pillows if they were not made from long chains of snap-rubber. There was little hair on his arms. Surprisingly little. Black hair reached up his back and stomach to his chest and the back of his neck and head to meet a full black beard and head of hair, but his arms were bare. He stepped towards the appointed ground and the other man fell into place. Daddy saw his opponent for the first time. He was unmoved. He did not hate this man. He walked towards him and boxed him and when it was over he heard measured applause and was taken over to a blue Peugeot behind the crowds and given from its boot a zipped duffle bag full of dirty cash.

Those men must have been satisfied by something they saw there. The gambling obscured the real pleasure. The cash had to be present, of course, to make it safe. To make it about business. To underpin the spectacle with something serious. To justify the performance. But if it was money they wanted there were other ways to get it and if it were a matter of business the fight would not have been with bare hands.

Yes, it was during this summer in the woods, before the new house was built, that Daddy told us these stories, confided in us, and Cathy and I listened like we were receiving precious heirlooms. Daddy's eyes became wide when he spoke to us, flecked, light blue, like worn denim, and he would lean in and open them generously then pinch them closed ever so slightly when he reached for a memory that was not quite clear. He sat forward in his chair with his long, thick legs apart, his elbows resting above his knees and his cavernous chest bearing broad, weighted shoulders.

I supposed that was how we made our money. From Daddy's fighting. But for months there would be no fights and Daddy would find other work. He mentioned this other work but there were fewer stories. The men he worked with on these jobs were sometimes travellers but more often they were from further away.

On one Thursday evening in our first September Cathy and I were sitting alone in our kitchen in the new home. It had been a windy afternoon and it was a windier evening. The foundations and joints of the house were tested for the first time and they creaked and groaned as they do in any building that has not yet set. The house was finding its position in the landscape, sitting down and relaxing into its trough, and we felt it sigh and moan for hours.

Daddy had been away since the afternoon before and we had not expected to see him again for days. We were surprised, then, when he came home that next morning just after dawn, while we were playing cards and drinking mugs of tea. We heard his car arrive outside, rolling then braking gently atop the leaf litter, and his familiar footsteps coming to us. I ran out to the hall to open the door for him, unbolting it at the top and bottom then turning the key. I pulled it in and stood aside to let my Daddy past. He walked to the kitchen table, alert but exhausted, and sat on one of the three wooden chairs that bent under his weight.

He pressed Cathy for a cup of tea and she got up and shifted the kettle back onto the stove. Daddy stretched his legs under the table then pulled them back in towards himself to make a start on tightly knotted bootlaces. Cathy rolled him a cigarette while waiting on the water and when she handed it to him I saw that her face was suddenly awake, like his, like he had brought something bright and alive home for us to devour. This night, as at other times, I saw that she was truly his daughter.

He had been called up by a lad, he said. Somebody he knew from here and there. Peter had lived in the village since he was nine or ten when his mother had moved from Doncaster to work at the chip shop, taking the customers' money then wrapping up the fish that the men fried. Peter had asked, through a friend of course, if Daddy could go over there to see him. He had heard that we had moved in nearby. That is to say, he had heard of Daddy's reputation.

Amongst certain types in the Yorkshire ridings and in Lincolnshire and in the counties around there were few who had not.

Peter had worked as a labourer on and off for the building companies in the area. Most had pulled back their work now and if it was not entirely dead then it was at least tethered. For two or more years Peter did not have much, Daddy told us. He had come through though. He had started to work for himself, privately, hiring himself out to anyone around who still had money. He built extensions, saw to bits of plumbing and knocked through sash windows. That sort of thing. Work that Daddy could have done but chose not to. Peter had been good at it, Daddy said. He had known how to manage his time and his money, which is half of anything. People spoke to their friends about him and he got more than enough work. For a time he did more than just live. There was pride, or something like it, and that was an almost-forgotten feeling in these parts. There became such things as futures and pasts and Peter began to take his place between them.

Two winters ago, he had taken a job at one of the big farms. He was building an extension to one of the outhouses when a fat dairy cow with two calves in her belly pulled her teats from the mechanical milking vice, kicked herself free from her trusses and galloped out the barn door. She knocked the ladder from beneath Peter's feet and he fell down beneath her hooves. She felt her grounding change as a hind leg found the soft lower back of the fallen man and she struck out against the outhouse wall then against Peter's head and neck. He was knocked out and lay bleeding on the filthy, wet cement.

Farms can be lonely places. They can be lonely places to have skin torn and bones crushed. They can be lonely places to die. But not for Peter that day. One of the permanent hands found him and his broken body and wrapped him in his coat and took him to Doncaster hospital in the back of a horse box.

Peter no longer had use of his legs. He had to spend most of his time in a wheelchair. He could no longer work. He stopped going to the pub of an evening. He stayed in his house, waiting for visitors. Old friends still dropped by but he had disappeared from view so all but the best began to forget him. The council did a bit and so did the church. Peter had an elderly neighbour who helped him with the garden. She cut branches from the trees and bushes at the right times of year and swept the fallen petals and the fallen leaves and made sure the water was able to run down the drains after it rained. He had an aunt that he had come to know since his mother died and she brought cakes and newspapers and changed his bed sheets every other Sunday.

Things were all right but they could have been better. After his accident, Peter had had to call in the money he was owed for jobs from the previous year and for materials he had supplied. He had not needed immediate payment before because things were good for him. His situation was steady. He had trusted that he would be paid like he trusted his own body and resolve. He had not considered that he might be cheated because he had never understood weakness. Our world was about muscle, Daddy always said, and for the first time in his life Peter did not have it. He had called round and half had paid straight away or had begun to pay in instalments. He had called again and half of the rest had come through too. The remaining debtors paid up with a bit of persistence and some harsh words from other men, from friends of Peter's from his childhood or working life. One debtor remained. He was a greasy bastard, said Daddy, from one of the big detached houses in the nicer part of Doncaster that had windows on both sides of the front door and a drive laid over with stones not concrete. He was not a good man, Daddy told us, and though he had got his money in plain sight of the law, he had not won it cleanly, nor had he worn it well. Not fairly nor honestly. He had not earned it by himself and with his wits and graft but with a league of other men, conspiring together to squeeze the remaining blood from their home town. This man had bought and sold other men's labour and owned dark clubs down dark alleys where women took off their clothes and danced. His money came from other people's bodies, Daddy told us, men's muscles and women's skin.

Peter had built a conservatory for him. It was a beautiful thing, by all accounts. It had taken weeks and cost a fortune and Peter was still owed nearly five thousand pounds and a set of precision power tools he had left on site. He had called and written and shouted from the street but the man had felt no need to respond. And so, after months, and after the rapid onset of poverty, Peter had asked around, and a friend of a friend of a friend had told him about the bearded giant that lived in the woods with his little son and hawkish daughter.

'I went up to see him yesterday afternoon,' said Daddy. 'He still lives in his mother's house, which I knew from years back when I used to live round there and mowed all lawns on that street. He told me all this. Gave me details. Put forward his case, so to speak. Well, he put it in such a way I were persuaded. You two know better than any I don't fight for nowt. And I'm not talking about money or prizes here. With this sort of fight there has to be a reason, and Pete had one. This Mr Coxswain owed him properly, and you know I don't like to see it. A man in Pete's position taken advantage of like that, brought lower when he's already low. I'm not a thug, I won't have you thinking that but by God it makes me angry. Pete told me where Coxswain would be and when. Most nights he drinks and plays cards at a back-room casino on edge of town. It's owned by an old colleague of his and pair of them set place up to make money for their lot. Coxswain takes home thousands some nights from desperate fools who don't understand they're fated to lose. I went then, on that same night when I knew he'd be there because I knew he'd have money on him. There'd be no point in going and doing all that I needed to do and at end of it coming away without Pete's cash. It's only half justice, you see. Other half is living. Getting done what needs to be done.'

Daddy had drunk his tea before it had cooled.

'So I borrowed Pete's car. He said to do that and he were right to. If car was seen it would be linked to him but nobody would think he could have done owt like what I were about to do. Pete can't even drive it any more, poor man. But nobody were going to see anyway. I parked ten minutes away and went to casino near two o'clock that morning and waited until after four, until after most of men had left, careful not to be seen, standing in cover of some plane trees. Well, Coxswain were one of last to leave. Tired but not drunk. Too alert for that. And too set on winning game. He came out to his car, which were parked near me. I'd have liked to have said I planned it that way – I should have – but I admit I were lucky. I were slow though. He opened boot and put his bag inside and I only got to him as he were closing it. He of course turned round, of course wondering who I were, guessing rightly that I were trouble for him, but not understanding why. Not then. He squared up but I started with a question first. Asked him if he were who I thought he were. He should have said no but he said that he were. Brave. A small amount of respect crept in. But then he messed up. Showed his true self. I asked for money he owed Pete. I asked for exact amount – I'm no thief. I said I'd take it to him. Made it clear I'd be taking it that evening and that I knew he had money on him. At first I thought he were doing all right. He said he were getting it from boot, and he went to open it. Men other than me might have been more suspicious, but I don't have time for that. I don't need to be suspicious. Suspicion comes from fear, see. If he'd pulled out a gun or knife I'd have known how to handle it. I'm not fussed. He opened up boot as if to get his bag of cash, but instead brought out a golf club. He lifted it. He tried to take it to me, but . . .'

Daddy looked down at the scrubbed oak table. A slight smile shifted his wet lips. Then he raised his blue eyes to Cathy. She had listened to the story but seemed unmoved. Her expression was mute, her eyes were clear.

'Well. It dindt matter,' he said. Cathy's irises widened then narrowed like the bobbing designs on an old spinning top.

Daddy told us what he had done next. He recounted how he had put up his arm to catch the club. How he had bent it in half with his two bare hands. How Mr Coxswain had ended up sprawled and choking on the tarmac, beaten so badly he should have been unconscious. But Daddy was expert in the consequences of time. He knew how to lengthen an engagement. He knew how to make a man suffer.

He detailed it all. Told us everything. Until it seemed like tears were coming to my eyes.

Then he stopped. Stopped suddenly. He rose from his chair and wrapped me in his arms, said he was sorry and that he should not have told us anything.

'You got Peter's money, then?' Cathy asked.

He turned back to her and sat down, still gripping my hand.

'I did,' he said. 'I did and I gave it back to him. All of it. And I'll show you what he gave me in return.'

Daddy raised himself onto his feet and slipped through the front door. He returned cradling two black puppies in his huge, bloodied hands. Two lurchers. Greyhounds crossed with border collies. We named them Jess and Becky that morning and made a snug den for them in the hallway. No floor had yet been laid in that room so it would be like outside and inside at the same time. Daddy said that would suit them.

Chapter Two

Daddy let us drink and smoke and after the shell of the house was built we spent long evenings sipping mugs of warm cider and puffing on the cigarettes that Cathy rolled. We listened to the radio and read to Daddy. Cathy in particular, in her deep steady voice that picked out the words and sentences that most needed hearing. When we were younger we had begged him for a television but Daddy said we were better off without it.

That was before we moved to the wood. It was before that summer of camping and before the new house was built. We lived further to the north, then, on the outskirts of a small town on the North Sea coast in a house that had been built amongst others of its kind in the 1930s. It was a semi-detached, of sorts. It could have been a row of back-to-back terraces in any other town but these houses were built like suburban three-beds, only smaller and with little care given to the gardens. Our older neighbours had planted purple and yellow pansies in thin borders between their lawns and the paths and privet hedges that cut them up, but most of the gardens on our street were patchy and muddy, held in place by dandelions and thistles.

Garden furniture was scarce but children's toys littered the ground every few houses along. I remember well a small plastic dolly with blonde curls lying face down in the mud of the front garden of the house on the corner, her pink cotton frock hitched up around her ears. I remember her lying there, untouched, for years while the rain and soil stained her body.

Some of the houses were coated in pebble-dash. Cathy and I liked these. We used to reach out and pick the sharp little stones from the cement as we scraped past, down the alley in between two houses and out into the fields beyond. The pock marks on the walls accumulated but most people did not look to see them and Cathy and I never concentrated on a single patch but released stones from here and there, careful not to form patterns with our picking. Our house in this estate was not covered with pebbledash. You could see the bricks from which it was made, those dark bloody-brown bricks. Our garden was neither untidy nor decorated. The grass was longer than the grass on other lawns and a darker green, but it was not wild. The concrete path led to a concrete step then the door, which was at first painted a royal blue then later a royal green which then, in turn, began to chip and reveal the blue, once more, beneath.

The hall presented a dark red carpet whose faded gold design took the eye from right to left, creeping over the worn middle to the plump edges and back again. It was like a vine or a climbing plant, its roots just outside the front door, had crept inside and up the stairs. When I was very small I pretended the pattern was a network of roads and I would trace my finger along it.

After the stairs, at the far end of the hall, the springy red carpet gave way to linoleum and a chipped MDF kitchen. We cooked with gas then, and Daddy used to light his cigarettes from the blue hissing flame and take them out into the back garden to finish. Off the hall also came a single living room that stretched the length of the house and there were three bedrooms and a bathroom upstairs.

In all, I lived there for fourteen years.

Back then, Daddy was with us sometimes but at other times he was not. We lived with Granny Morley. She loved us well, cooked for us and washed our clothes. There were always two varieties of vegetable with our dinner and she used enough washing powder to make our clothes clean but not so much that it clung to the cotton and made us itch. While we were at school she hoovered the carpets and dusted the shelves and went down to the high street to Mr Evans' butcher shop, the Costcutter, the greengrocer's and Margaret's Hair Salon, where she met her friends every Thursday afternoon.

On the weekends or after school Granny Morley made sure we played outside in the garden or in the fields behind the house. Sometimes we went down to the beach and played in the caves and rock pools. She was a loving woman, our Granny, but she was distant. Sometimes she looked right through us. Sometimes she seemed to catch onto sounds in the next room or outside when we tried to speak to her, like she could hear something we could not. She raised her head and tilted it and as she did she lifted a hand to the arm of her chair or the sofa.

When we were small Granny Morley walked us to school, holding one of each of our hands in each of hers. Our school was in the town itself on the other side of an area of parkland where seagulls the size of small dogs pulled scraps from bins. We went through there to school in the mornings in our uniforms. Red sweatshirts, white polo shirts and grey flannel trousers or pleated skirts for Cathy and black leather shoes that we polished every Sunday evening.

The main part of the school was in an old red-brick Victorian building and there was a bell tower at one end. The bell was too rusty to chime and nobody ever thought to fix it. Instead there were red bells like fire alarms attached to the walls of the class-rooms inside and those told us when to go out to play and when to come back inside. Some of the corridors had bright pictures stuck to the wall with tac and some did not. The whole place smelt of OXO cubes and sugar paper.

I kept myself to myself in the early years. I walked around and around the playground pretending to scale great mountain ranges or horizontal marsh-lands. In the summer months I sat beneath a sycamore tree on the edge of the school field. I collected insects in my hands only to release them at the end of playtime or lunch hour. Daddy asked me if I wanted an insect collecting set for my birthday or some jars to put them in to and take them home but I said I did not. I liked having them in my hands for that certain amount of time then letting them go off again into the undergrowth, back to their homes and to their lives. I would think about them living those lives while I sat back in my chair in the class-room and gazed blankly at times-tables.

Cathy organised games and I joined in with those. When I was about six and she was eight she got into a barney with three of the lads in her year. Adam Hardcastle, Callum Gray and Gregory Smowton. Possibly it was the kind of event that only seems important to those involved but even then I wondered whether the others spent as much time thinking on it as I have. Over the years I must have spent whole days with this memory in my mind, closing my eyes and trying to walk into different parts of the scene, trying to gauge where each person was in each moment, trying to hear how fast each of their hearts was beating. I must have spent minutes squinting into the distance of it, trying to see this boy's face when he knew he could not hold on any more, trying to catch onto the exact words my sister had used when she described the bits I had not seen.

I wondered if she thought about it too. Or if the boys did. Or if any of the other small people at the far reaches of my recollection spent the time that I had thinking about the bits in which they played a part. It seems to me that so much of everything came from this, and that if anyone thought about moments like this enough, the future would be done before it had even started, and I mean that in a good way.

She was tall for her age, Cathy, and strong and fit. She had cropped black hair that she tucked behind her ears and blue eyes like Daddy's. Adam, Callum and Gregory all came from the row of tall terraced houses near the school, with pointed roofs and protruding windows. They wore a new pair of brightly coloured trainers each term. They all supported Manchester United even though we lived in Yorkshire, and they had the team kits to prove it. They always had the widest range of football stickers or pogs and their pretty mothers collected them from the school gates on time every day and dropped them off the next morning with a pack-up of sandwiches, jammy dodgers and sweet cartons of apple juice that got sweeter with the heat from the classroom and the morning sun.

I suppose it is normal for little boys to tell little girls that they are not allowed to play with them but I suppose most little girls know what the answer will be from the start and do not bother to ask. Cathy, of course, did ask, and was told. She asked again and she was told again. She said it was not fair but was told by Gregory Smowton that it was his ball so he could choose who played and who did not. She tried to play anyway. She placed herself on the field in what seemed like the right position and when the ball came near she ran for it. She got it. But then what happened next was more difficult. She was not on either of the teams and so had no idea which direction to take, to whom to pass, nor which goal to run for. I remember her just standing there with the ball and the boys standing too, not knowing too whether to tackle her or to ask for a pass, and her looking startled then suddenly realising that she did not want it anyway.

Part of me still wishes that she had run with it somewhere, ducked and dived round all the lads and kicked it straight past the goalie between the rucksack posts. In my mind she would have been a footballing sensation. But in the event nobody ever saw her play. She stood there by the ball then she walked away. Walked away over to the other side of the field. She told me later when I asked her that she knew it would always be their game. Even if she played, and even if she played well, it would always be their game.

She had caught their attention though. She had riled them. For the rest of that term they sought her when she was alone. They took her aside and punched and kicked her and sometimes strangled her and she ran away or resisted quietly. She pushed their hands off or blocked their blows when they came at her. But she did nothing decisive. Nothing that would end it. And because the boys had no ultimate reason to stop, and because it was fun and made them feel better, they continued. Several weeks passed and they would still chase her behind the bins and beat her or find her in the park between the school and our house or sometimes down at the beach where she and I would wade about in the rock-pools.

There was a trigger though. Something shifted in her mind. I do not know whether it was the particular action or whether it was that I was involved, but it was something.

It was a Friday. It was the Friday before Good Friday. School had broken up for the Easter holidays the day before. The first day we had to ourselves was dry but there was such a strong wind coming in off the North Sea that the air was wet with salty water. It whipped our faces so that they were near red raw and the salt combed our hair and dug under our fingernails.

We went down to the beach to look for hermit crabs. We picked up shells and tried to see if there was one inside. When there was we looked for a moment and placed it back then looked again, creating a map in our minds so as not to disturb the same creature twice.

We both saw the boys coming from a long way off. They made no attempt to disguise themselves. They stretched out their bodies and swung their arms as they walked. I could tell Gregory from his red hat. One of the others had a football. He kicked it hard and the ball scuffed over the sand and stopped twenty metres away for him to lazily walk after it and meet it. It splashed through shallow saltwater puddles and tossed dark wet sand this way and that.

Cathy saw them too but she did not stop. She picked out a beautiful little shell and asked me with a steady voice if I had seen it before. I told her that I had not and she turned it over to look inside. There was nothing there. The animal that had grown the shell was long dead and no little crab had crawled into its grave. She bent down and placed it back amongst the seaweed.

The salty gusts were hitting hard from over the North Sea. Cathy's hair, black as Whitby jet, whipped about her as she stood up to face the boys. The toggles of her coat beat against each other, sounding the sweet wooden pulse of a marimba being struck by the wind. I watched her the whole time. I could not take my eyes off her. I was ever her witness.

Adam Hardcastle ran in and knocked her to the wet sand. She put her arms back to break her fall but did not make to get up and he soon had her held down. Callum and Gregory walked over, casually.

None of them seemed to notice me though I had been standing right beside my sister. I was younger and small for my age so I knew I could not have done anything except get help. I turned and started running across the sands. Daddy was not in town but I could tell Granny Morley and she could get word to him or else to other people she knew, other people who were a bit like Daddy.

I had not gone twenty metres before Callum caught on to the neck of my sweatshirt and pulled me back. Gregory had begun slapping my sister gently across the face. He then reached down to the bottom of her polo shirt and pulled it up and placed his left hand on the right side of her chest, on her nipple. She was just a girl and there was nothing there but bone and muscle but perhaps he thought this would bother her. He held his hand there and she just stared at him. There was no reason to her why this was worse or different from what had gone on before. She had no idea that Gregory was acting out a kind of play, taking his cues from things he had either seen or heard, doing something that he thought would be worse for her – the worst thing of all. But she did not know. She had not been told yet. She was not in on the game. All she felt was a cold wet hand on her skin that was no worse than a kick in the teeth.

Gregory challenged her on it. 'Aren't you bothered?' He could not understand why she remained unmoved. 'Slut,' he said. She stared at him. 'You should be bothered by me touching you here,' he said.

It was not working. He turned to me. I was hanging limply in Callum's arms.

'Dunk his head in that pond,' said Gregory. Callum laughed cruelly and dragged me over to a rock pool.

The first time he pushed my head into the cold water I saw a single sea anemone clinging desperately to the side of the jagged crevice, infringed upon on each side by a colony of chipped barnacles.

The second time I saw two distinct types of seaweed and what I thought was a razor clam.

I remember these things. These were the things I promised myself I would remember.

The third time my head did not reach the water. Behind me, my sister had risen up from the sand kicking and screaming my name and their names and her name. She had fought them all and won and they were now legging it back to town with their football left behind. She pulled me up and told me to run all the way home. She told me to run home and stay there and to tell Granny Morley that she would not be long but that it might be a good idea to get Daddy. She wanted Daddy. She left me there and ran off behind the boys. She chased them down and I knew she would catch them all. Her legs were longer and stronger than theirs in those days. I turned and ran home and did what she said.

The boys were fine. After she was finished with them they were bruised and tender but they were not seriously hurt. She did not know how to cause too much damage to a human body and their wounds healed quickly. In school for the weeks that followed they kept themselves away from Cathy and for some time they kept away from everybody. When the new term came they were more or less as they had been before, in the way they walked and the way they spoke to people. If there was any more humility than before or any more regard for other people, it was hidden.

In the immediate aftermath of the fight one of the boys told his mother about what had happened. Or part of what had happened. He told his mother that he and Adam and Gregory had been set upon by that feral girl with the strange, absent father. His mother had gone into the school to tell the headmistress.

The following day, Daddy was summoned to go in and speak with the headmistress. He had come back within two hours of Granny Morley's call and sat me on his knee as we waited for Cathy. Granny Morley asked him if he was going to go out looking for her but he said that he had already seen her out on the beach. He said she was sitting on her own and would come home when she was ready.

Cathy was ready at around six o'clock in the evening. She had been out on the beach all night and all day. Her hands and forearms were covered in a thin layer of sand and there was a small amount of blood on her knuckles. The sand together with the blood looked like the thin lines of grimy oil that wash up on North Sea beaches and mark the high tide.

Daddy got up and took hold of one of her hands. He led Cathy to the seat next to his. He asked her what happened.

She looked at him and I saw that there were tears in her eyes. They were hardly there at all, having not yet pooled into salty droplets, but I could tell the difference. Like the difference between lit and unlit black or between a dead thing and an alive thing.

At first she did not respond. She sat in silence. We all did. Daddy did not ask her again and neither did Granny Morley nor I say anything.

After almost a minute her chest began to convulse. I thought that she was hiccoughing but the heaving became more rapid and then the tone changed and she let the tears come all at once. A deluge.

She sobbed. Her breathing was like waves building up then dropping suddenly over a sea wall. She exhaled as if through an harmonica.

As she cried she spoke: 'I felt so helpless, Daddy. I felt as if there wandt owt I could do that would change them. Or hurt them. Not really hurt them like they were hurting me. I could hit them all I liked but it woundt change a thing. They were so nasty to me, Daddy. Not the pain, Daddy, I dindt mind that, but the way they made me feel inside. No matter what I do, I can never win.'

'You did though. You fought them and beat them.

You protected your little brother. What more could you do?'

Daddy ran his hands through his hair and then his beard as if searching for an answer there.

'I mean it doendt matter, does it? I mean that things will always be as they are now. I mean that there will always be more fights and it will just get harder and harder. I feel like I'll never just be left alone.'

Daddy continued to stroke his hair. He looked more concerned than I had ever seen him. 'Did you think to tell the teacher?' he asked. 'Did you think to tell teacher what these boys were doing?'

'I did,' Cathy replied, 'but she told me they were nice boys.'

It was because of this, I think, that Daddy took us all into the headmistress's office together. He led Cathy and I by our hands through the narrow corridors of our school. The ceilings were low and lit by halogen strip bulbs that flickered and shone the same colour as the magnolia paint on the walls, making it appear as if the light were emanating from the plaster. The only windows were long and thin and tucked just beneath the ceiling, well above the heads of the children who walked up and down these corridors so that when they looked up and out into the world beyond all they could see was the sky. On that day the sky was a mesh of criss-crossed grey and white cords being ripped and tugged and frayed by colliding winds.

To get to Mrs Randell's office we walked to the end of the corridor and up a flight of stairs. They were the only stairs in the single-storey school and opened onto a landing holding doors to her office, the staffroom and the administrative office where we collected our lunch tokens each week and handed in consent forms for us to go on school trips.

Daddy knocked. It was a heavy fire door painted dark blue with a small, square window made from thick glass with a network of thin, black wires running through it to hold the shards together in case of breakage. His fat knuckles made a dull thump against the wood, a sound that was echoed by Mrs Randell's dampened voice from inside the room, instructing us to enter.

Her voice or the instructions she issued sharpened as Daddy opened the door and she told us to sit down. She sat in a high-backed chair behind a large pine veneer desk and there were three chairs set opposite her, made from moulded plastic with a thin, course cushion glued to each seat. I sat on the right, Cathy sat on the left and Daddy was in the middle.

Mrs Randell looked comfortable. She looked as

if she led a comfortable life. She wore a peach linen suit and her hair was both blonde and brown. Or blonde overlaid onto brown. It descended just below her ears and flicked out to the sides.

She seemed good enough (as good as could be expected) but she had only known comfort. And she looked troubled by us. Perhaps she would have preferred it if Cathy had never beaten those boys or if Callum's mother had not told her about it so she would not have to be sitting there on a Friday afternoon having a conversation about violence.

It was cool outside but her office was hot. The central heating was on and the windows shut. There were piles of heavily typed documents on her desk and the sideboard and walls bore the varied compositions of sundry children in oversized scrawls and motley hues. There was a row of rubber stamps stained with carmine ink. Each sported a slogan of adulation and acclaim.

'I hope you know that your daughter's behaviour was unacceptable. The attack was unprovoked. Those poor boys just wanted to play football on the beach and they asked Cathy if she and Daniel wanted to join in. I mean, I know Daniel and Cathy might not have had quite the same opportunities in life as Gregory, Adam and Callum but that's no excuse for behaviour such as hers. Gregory had bruises all up his legs and Callum's mother said the boys had even been kicked in their private parts. She must be told that it's not acceptable to kick little boys there.'

Mrs Randell went on like this and Daddy said nothing much in response. Neither did Cathy. A viscous silence had settled on Daddy and Cathy and me and although Mrs Randell spoke in fluid phrases that rippled against and sporadically punctured the gummed ambience, drab quiet was the primary mood and her dry utterances did little to refine that mood. Later, Daddy told us that after he had heard the teacher's comments on the conduct of the boys he saw that there would be no real use in responding with his true thoughts. Mrs Randell's assessment was simply the way people saw things, he told us. It was the way the world was and we just had to find methods of our own to work against it and to strengthen ourselves however we could.

Outwardly, Daddy agreed with Mrs Randell's recommendations and offered an apology on behalf of his daughter. He proffered assurances that it would not happen again. He insisted that discipline would be enforced at home and that Cathy would find a way to appease the boys.

Daddy walked us back home through the darkening suburbs to Granny Morley's house. He told us that he would be staying for at least a month and that we should come home from school on time every day so that we could all spend time together.

He told Cathy that she had done everything correctly. He only wished she had acted sooner.

Granny Morley died on a Tuesday afternoon. Cathy found her in her usual chair in the sitting room and closed all the curtains and all the doors and forbade my entrance. We had no way of contacting Daddy so we just kept that room shut and the curtains closed and lived upstairs in near-silent vigil. Cathy snuck down for food from the cupboards. We lived off biscuits and bananas and crisps until Daddy happened to come home a week and a half later and we ran to him and wept for the first time and he told us that he would never, not ever, leave us again.

II

Years later and miles away that girl's brother trudges through mud to find her. It has been days. I have seen no trace but I still have hope.

The memory of that evening in our house in the copse does not loosen. The stills do not fall from their reel. Each face and each gesture confirms its shape. Nothing slackens.

As I walk I think on the sight of them all. I think on my sister with her slick of black hair. I think on my Daddy and the words he did and did not speak. I think on the others, all eyeballs and teeth.

I was right to run.

As I walk now I look about. The further I step from home the more uncanny the sights become. My eyes respond in kind. They fall upon the familiar.

I see the chimney stack and cooling towers of a power station on the horizon, gorging on the earth and spewing measures of caustic exhaust. I see a veil of ashen smog that hangs between land and sky and the leaden vapour pooling into mock clouds. I see a chain of pylons stretching from far-ground to foreground like a vast, disarticulated arthropod, and tethered shadows, more gargantuan still, lying upon the hills like the insignia of pagan forbears. I see bovine silhouettes shift steadily across meadows, hulking their uneasy weight from trough to furrow, and elsewhere, I see the dusk settle on the fleeces of grazing ewes like sparks from flint to tinder. I watch the land glow and the sky burn. And I step through it with a judicious tread.

I pass from Elmet bereft.

Chapter Three

We kept on with our silly childhood games long after we were much too old. Our copse provided the materials we needed and an undulant terrain in which to run and hide. In another world we might have grown up faster, but this was our strange, sylvan otherworld, so we did not. And that, after all, was why Daddy had moved us here. He wanted to keep us separate, in ourselves, apart from the world. He wished to give us a chance of living our own lives, he said.

We played at archery, like we were outlaws in the wood. After the house was built and Daddy had more time, he showed us how to make bows and arrows for ourselves, and explained which were the best tools to use. We made longbows that were almost the height of each of us and whittled from a single piece of hardwood. There was a lot of ash about but oak was better, and yew the best, Daddy said. He would pick a piece that had the right shape and then we would strip away the bark, the soft new growth beneath it, and then cut it down with a lathe, only shaving off a little at each time in case we went too far. We made our arrows with materials from the woods around. When we practised with targets we made do with arrows with blunt ends as we shot them against a hessian sack with a painted bulls-eye. But when Daddy hunted birds or rabbits or muntjac he needed a hard metal tip and had to buy them.

We made bows that we could use easily now, bows that would test and strengthen us and bows that we would develop into. Cathy could pull much harder than me because her arms were so long, even though I had the broader chest, even then. She did not flinch when the arrow was released and the bow string whipped at her arm, as it can do when it is hard pulled, when you are tired or your arm is not properly aligned. Or when you have the kind of arms that are so thin and supple that when they are straightened to their limit the soft, fleshy part with the blue veins at the crook of your elbows is almost convex. Both Cathy and I had arms like these. You release the bowstring with all the power it took to pull it back, and as the arrow is loosed it slaps against your left forearm. This is not just a skin pain. It goes deeper. I did not have much else on me but skin and so it hurt me in my marrow. Those painful vibrations that send waves through your bone, and then further.

But Cathy did not seem to feel it or else she did not care. She never wore a leather armband around her forearm and always kept her arm as straight as she could, so as to keep her aim, and so inevitably, because of her supple, almost convex arms, she would pull the string back to its full extension and when it was released it would slap with a loud crack against her soft, pale skin. It went on like that, with Cathy holding the bow with her arm turned towards the string and loosing her arrows so that that she was struck hard, again and again. Her forearm became red raw and so bruised that the grey and yellow blood that settled there almost made a complete bracelet that seeped all the way around, like her skin was stained with gold.

Still, she did not alter her method. Daddy became angry with her every time he saw it. At least, he was angry in the manner that feeling is expressed when it is mixed with love. Like sadness but with the energy for intervention. He would go over to her and take the bow gently away and sit down with it some way off. He would wait for Cathy to calm down, to stop breathing so deeply with the exhaustion of it all, and for her to go and join him on the ground, amongst the leaf litter. I would go over too and Daddy would pull out some crackers and a block of hard cheese and we would sit and eat them together, and then go back to the house.

Chapter Four

There was a woman who lived down the way. Her house was maybe a mile and a half away but there was only one turning between our road and hers so that made her a neighbour. She lived alone in a white house that had a window on either side of the front door and in the summer months sweet peas grew on trellises along the side of the house. There was a garden to the front and at the back. She parked her dark blue car on one side and on the other side a farmer's field began where there were rows of dark cabbages followed by lines of beets.

Cathy and I were unsure of how she knew Daddy. We never understood why he knew anyone other than us, but they seemed reasonably acquainted, even though we were far from Granny Morley's home now and I thought everyone would be a stranger.

That first winter came early, and quickly too. One morning in November when it was so cold that crispy ice strangled the drainpipes and windowsills, Daddy got us up just after dawn, and we walked out towards Vivien's house, down the hill to our little lane and then along hers. I was wrapped up in two tartan scarves and a dark green fleece that I had zipped up to the top, and I held it tight against my chin to keep the warmth locked inside. Cathy had pulled thick purple walking socks up over the ankles of her jeans to shield her legs from the biting breeze and Daddy wore his usual coat with a woollen jumper underneath, and motorcycle gloves.

The walk down the hill was slippery as the frost on the soft tussocks melted beneath our feet, and we slid a few inches with each step. The morning smelt of wood and little else. The summer scents had been bottled by the cold. It was a clear day, though, particularly now when the sun was low, and bright rays cut raw across the grass. When we got to the path the trees cast long, precise shadows. The stones on the ground were not smooth but the kind chucked up by heavy machinery, and, little though they were, they sliced the light more precisely still.

We walked quickly to keep warm and I jogged on every few steps to keep up the pace. Cathy had been quiet since the previous evening but seemed to lighten as we lengthened our strides.

'How do we know her?' she asked Daddy.

'Through your mother.'

We could say nothing after he mentioned our mother. We almost never spoke of her and his mentioning her was so rare that we did not know whether to take it as an invitation or as a warning. I could not detect either mode in his tone nor read his expression. He walked on impassively, while I looked up at him then down again at the path in front of us then up again at him, like our eager dogs who trotted at our feet and turned their faces up to their masters on every other step. The dogs looked at me and Cathy. We looked at Daddy.

Becky, who never ran too far from me, slashed her tail against my shins as she hopped in front of my feet. I kept kicking her, accidentally, then stumbling on myself so as not to hurt her.

Vivien's garden had a neatness about it but looked natural. At first sight the ground was uneven and the rose bushes were strangled at the roots by shallow weeds but I saw that there were no fallen petals or dried leaves. Those had been cleared away. The grass stopped suddenly at the patio, trimmed severely at the edges to keep a clean line, parallel to a set of French windows.

Daddy knocked and Vivien opened the door and

stared at us. She was tall like Daddy, but slim. Her hair was a thick russet and her skin so pale that you could almost see the blood behind it, the redness at her cheeks and the blueness at her eyes. It was honest skin. It was the kind of skin that could not hide a mark or a blemish or a sickness that lay within. She looked tired, either a tiredness from the early morning or a tiredness from a long life. She was perhaps forty, but seemed both older and younger, with irises that were both a bright green and a dull yellow, and an uncertain stoop that you see in both old ladies and adolescent girls. In the moment she stared at us, she inhaled deeply and exhaled quickly, as if she were conjuring a beginning or marking an ending.

'I didn't expect you this early,' she said to Daddy, although her eyes still jumped between my sister and me. She turned to him now and smiled, and pulled the door wider to see us all better, and then to let us in.

Cathy took the invitation and stepped over the threshold, standing in front of the woman as she placed a long hand on each of Cathy's upper arms.

'You must be Catherine,' she said. 'I met you when you were a toddler and your brother was a baby.'

Vivien ushered Cathy through into the house and I took the step up into the hall.

She looked at me and took me as she had taken

Cathy, firmly and with both hands. 'Daniel. Come in.'

The sitting room was light despite the heavy green plants propped up on the windowsills. The French windows faced south-east towards the morning sun, and light poured in over the sharply edged papers that had been placed carefully on specific surfaces. There was a deep sofa covered by worn blue velvet, with two large sitting cushions. They dipped to meet each other in the middle but were still quite plump at their outer edges. There was a blanket on one of the arms with a scene stitched together with red and white wool but obscured by the folds. There was a carpet atop a carpet, one grey and fitted to the size and shape of the room, and one a set rectangle with tassels on the two shorter edges and a pattern of lines and angles that I would have sat down on and traced my fingers over were I younger or alone. There was a coffee table in the centre of the room and a round upright table by the French windows with a white cotton cloth and a tucked-in chair. There was a plate and a cup of tea or coffee on this table, and I supposed Vivien had eaten her breakfast there. There was a fireplace with a smoke-screen in front of it, and although there was a fire already made up, nothing had yet been lit. Fire tools were in a bucket on the hearth. Tongs. A poker. A shovel. A coarse brush. And triangles of compacted newspaper were stored in a small open-topped wicker chest, safely stowed in a corner away from the fireplace. There were some ornaments on the mantel, and I remember particularly a small clock with Roman numbers, whose face was set into a roughly hewn piece of limestone.

Daddy and Vivien came through into the sitting room to join Cathy and me. He had taken off his jacket and had his hands in his trouser pockets while she had hers crossed over her body with each hand on the opposite shoulder.

They were standing close to one another as if they were old friends but without the years of separation. There was the comfort of continuance between them. Yes, she was standing at his side but slightly in front, so that his arm could have been partially around her. I could not quite see but there might have been contact.

He opened his mouth. He looked particularly handsome today, within my own conception of what it was to be handsome, which I suppose came only from the image of my father.

'Vivien were a friend of your mother's,' said Daddy again, seriously. 'She's going to teach you things what I can't. She's good at things what I aren't. You'll be spending your mornings with her.'

Cathy and I did not mind taking orders from Daddy. Sometimes we were more like an army than a family and he was not the type of leader to make you do anything for nothing.

Vivien looked nervous. She only seemed half on board, half off board. As she looked between us, weakly, her pink lips became whiter and she pulled them into a smile.

Daddy looked better pleased with his plan. He clapped his hands together. 'Let's get going then. I'll be off for the next few hours. You can begin today.'

He turned and left the room. I heard a rustle in the hall as he picked his still-warm jacket off the coat stand and put it on. The door clicked shut after him.

Cathy's expression was sour and she eyed Vivien suspiciously. Vivien loosened her grip on her shoulders and walked over to the small round table by the windows, the one with the tea and cake crumbs. She untucked the chair and sat down. She looked at both of us, but still mainly at Cathy.

'I want to make these lessons, you know, fun for you both.'

I thought for a moment that she had said the wrong thing. Cathy stared. She did not raise her eyebrows or roll her eyes. She did not even purse her lips. She just stared. She felt as if she had been patronised. Slighted. I knew this because I knew my sister well, better than anyone, even Daddy, though he thought they were so alike in their hearts.

Vivien looked at Cathy seriously, unable to decipher the sudden silence.

But Cathy took Daddy deadly seriously in his attempts to train us against the world. She found a kind of solace in his tasks. She wanted to be every inch of him but believed what he said about how different she was, about how she had to be good at different things, how she had to find a different way of surviving. If Daddy thought Vivien's lessons were important then she would commit herself to them, at least initially.

So Cathy stopped staring and came back to life, throwing herself into the moment.

'What do we need to do, then?' Cathy asked.

Vivien ventured a smile.

That evening Cathy and I went out into the clearing we had lived in before Daddy had built the house. It was still well-trodden but the earth was harder than it had been during the summer and the branches of the overhanging trees were thin tendrils. We sat on the cold stumps of a couple of trees.

'I can't think of owt worse than growing up to be her,' Cathy said. She was talking about Vivien.

'I thought she was okay,' I replied. 'She's not very like us but I don't know if that matters.'

Cathy didn't answer me. She seemed sad, restless,

and she cradled her mug of warm tea and looked into the liquid.

We had come outside because Daddy was in a dark mood and had shut himself up in his room alone. He had been light and brisk all day but as the sun began to set just before five o'clock he had taken a turn for the worse and slipped out of the kitchen quietly. We had not noticed right away and kept on with making the dinner. It was only when we had put the scrubbed potatoes inside the oven to bake and turned to sit down that we noticed he had gone. Cathy went out into the hall to see if he wanted any beer or cider to drink before the dinner was ready but found that the door of his room was locked shut without any answer from within. She had come back and when the food was ready we had eaten alone, leaving a plate for him covered on the hob. He stayed locked away long after we had finished, and I suggested that we go outside.

Sometimes he did lock himself away like that but we never knew why. Of course we assumed that he was troubled by something and did not want to share it with us but we could never really know because we never saw. I never saw my father waver, never saw him lose control or stumble, and I took it for granted that I would never and could never see him cry. Perhaps he was different when he locked himself away. Perhaps he was more himself or less himself in those moments, whichever way you think of it. But I could not say for certain, because I never saw.

When Cathy did not reply to me I thought again about what she had said about Vivien, and tried to work out what she had meant by it. Sometimes she did just take against people. She told me exactly why they were bad people and she usually convinced me to feel the same way. She had not explained herself here and I was having trouble working it out.

'She wandt very welcoming,' I offered after a while. 'I mean, she was and she wandt. She was polite and helpful. As much as you'd expect. But she was always distracted, like she wanted us to leave.' Cathy said nothing and I thought again. 'And she seemed embarrassed by us. Not that there was anyone else there to see that we were there with her. Nobody else to question our involvement with her. But she seemed uncomfortable and it was the kind of uncomfortable you feel when you're embarrassed not when you're unsettled or unprepared. It was like even though there weren't any other people there to feel ashamed in front of, she felt them there anyway and she dindt want those invisible people to see her talking to us.'

'That's not the thing I was thinking of. It's the way she moves around. The way she walks. Hers is the most horrible body I've ever seen. She can't move forwards without moving sideways. It's her hips. She's not even fat. There's no extra weight on her, but her hip bones are so large and wide that she can't move without considering them. When she walks she has to follow their lead and they sway from side to side. God, it's disgusting. Can you imagine running with hips like that? Can you imagine trying to run away from someone when you're being pulled back by your own bones? Can you imagine what tops of your legs must feel like being stuck in to hips like that? Muscles on your thighs being twisted as you're trying to run away and your knees trying to support those hips and your running thighs while trying to keep them in line with your feet. All of you trying to go forwards and bloody bones are holding you back. Jesus fucking Christ, I'd rather die.'

She continued. 'Do you remember that time we were down by canal, Daniel? I can't even remember which town it were or what year only that you had that white T-shirt with orange setting sun on it that Granny Morley brought you back from that holiday she went on – only holiday I ever remember her going on – and so you must have been about eight because you grew so quickly after that – when you were nine and ten – that you coundt have fitted into that T-shirt after that age. Maybe it were Sheffield we were in but I can't remember. It doendt matter. We were there together, alone, because Daddy was somewhere else. Probably fighting outside of town.

'Anyway,' she said. 'We were down by canal, Daniel. Me and you, alone. We walked as sun went down and we saw that lady sitting under bridge with her knees up and the palms of each hand cradling each side of her face like her own cheeks were softest things she'd ever touched and like she were touching them for first time. We walked past her under bridge and there were sick on ground and ashes that handt singed anything but were lying on top of paving stones. Her handbag were on ground too and were open with tissues and lipsticks and that falling out and she handt even noticed, let alone stopped to pick any of it up. There were a smell of grass that had been trod on and rotted, and a smell of dogs. And that man in background. Do you remember man in background? Almost fully hidden by shadows of bridge? Standing on mud behind paving stones?'

'I don't remember seeing either of them,' I said. And I did not. But I did remember the news later that week that a woman had gone missing and that she was last seen going down to the towpath. And I remember my sister telling us that we had seen the woman and that there had been a man behind her.

'But you believe me?' she implored.

'Yes, of course I believe you.'

'And you believe I was right? That it were man behind lurking in the shadows who did for her? Who pushed her in?'

I looked her in the eye. The police had searched for Jessica Harman, nineteen, for weeks before finding her tucked away by a weir, miles downstream. When they found the body and identified her they concluded that it had been a natural death. They said that she had been intoxicated and had accidentally stumbled into the canal on her way home and that the current, buoyed by recent flooding, had carried her away. They had come to this conclusion before they had found her, however. It was based on the fact that she had been out drinking with friends that evening. The police had looked for people who might have tried to kill her but decided that there was no one with a motive. Then they had found the body and decided that their assumption had been confirmed. But Cathy was sure that she had seen the woman and also a man and that Jessica Harman had been pushed.

Two weeks later a student was found washed up further along the canal by one of the locks. This time it was a boy, and it was thought that he had fallen in drunkenly, too, or else had killed himself. But we spoke again of the middle-aged man Cathy had seen in the shadow of the bridge and how easy it would be for a stealthy stranger to ease a person on their way. It would be so little like murder. Just a gentle nudge at somebody who was already unsteady. A stranger. Unless you were seen you could never be caught.

And so Daddy had asked around at Cathy's behest. He found nothing but continued to search all the same. He patrolled the canals at night for weeks and weeks but did not come across anything out of the ordinary. He said if there had been a murderer lying in wait for young women, he had scared him off.

Of course we did not go to the police. Neither Cathy nor I had even suggested it. There was little trust there. No love lost.

But we had all believed Cathy.

Chapter Five

There was a cold spell in the week before Christmas. With the cold I became sluggish. Usually eager to help Daddy with his work outside, I spent more and more time in the kitchen, taking for myself the jobs that allowed me to stay indoors. I made sure the stove was well stoked every day and the chopped wood in the store was piled high so it did not have to be topped up from outside too often. I cleaned the house and baked cakes and mince pies for Christmas Day. Daddy went to the shop in the village and bought sheets of paper in gold and silver and red, white and green and I set about cutting them up and folding and gluing them into decorations.

I sat at the kitchen table and made snowflakes as I had at school. I cut circles and folded them into quarters and inserted apertures and grooves so when they were unravelled they became tiny sheets of falling ice, jagged but symmetrical. The gold paper became stars. I made the shapes of trees with the green paper. Winter trees. I copied the few pines that we had in the copse, the only ones that still held green. From those trees, Daddy brought in branches of green needles and pinecones for making wreathes, which I constructed as best I could, approximating those I had seen on Christmas cards.

'You're a funny lad,' Daddy said to me on the morning of Christmas Eve. It was nearly nine o'clock and he had been awake and working for several hours. He had seen to the chickens and walked the puppies, who were now burly adolescents, frayed at the edges, with chalky incisors and too-long limbs. It had snowed overnight and Daddy had shovelled it into piles that now looked like an oddly dispersed mountain range. The puppies had made a scattering of deep paw prints in the snow and were now scaling these new summits.

'Why am I funny?' I asked.

'Don't know. You like making house nice and that.'

He drew back a chair from the table to sit down and I got up to pour coffee from the pot I had sitting atop the stove. Our coffee was always made slowly, brewed on the hob for hours, well-stewed, bitter, smoky. That is how we liked it.

67

I made my Daddy a hearty breakfast and then he went out again into the cold.

I spent the morning continuing to make paper decorations and then I stuck them up around the house. I slotted some of the shapes in the tiny gaps between the window frames and the panes of now naturally frosted glass. I stuck others on cupboards or propped them up on shelves or in picture frames. I hung paper chains of gold, silver, red, green, white – made from scraps and offcuts – from hooks on the ceiling of the kitchen which Daddy had originally pinned up to hang dried meat.

Daddy did not come back for lunch. This was unusual, especially on such a cold day. At one point I peered out the window to see if he was on his way, but he was not and I served up the vegetable soup I had made for me and Cathy anyway. We briefly remarked on Daddy's absence but other than that the meal passed in contented silence.

As the afternoon proceeded and it started to fall dark, I began to worry. It was not that it was late. It was not yet four o'clock and it was that time of year when it seemed to get dark again almost before I could say I was truly awake. But it was rare for Daddy to stay out all day until dusk without coming home once for a bite to eat. If not lunch, then cake or an oat biscuit. And it was Christmas Eve. I had prepared a feast of hot pies and braised onions to keep us going until tomorrow when our main meal was to be goose. Cathy had stayed in especially and practised carols on her violin. Her bow strokes bounced over the strings, more like she was playing a sea shanty than a hymn, but I could recognise the melodies nonetheless and hummed along when she really got into her stride, lifting my voice to its full extent where I knew the words.

When darkness fell completely I thought about going with a torch to find him but the world outside was huge and everything looked different in the snow. Even though I already knew the copse well, I could not be certain I would be able to find my way through it with just a small light held in my hand, reflecting off the bright white that obscured the familiar colours and the precise shapes of the landscape. And I could not be sure that Daddy was in the copse. That is where he usually went, but not always. And although he had said he had got work to finish up there he also said he would not be long.

I thought about the tools he used out in the woods. Sharp axes and machetes and saws. I had a vision of him slipping suddenly and cutting open his thigh, where the thick, deep arteries ran, and of him passing out in the cold, his blood at first melting the snow around then freezing again within it.

I had already put on my coat and boots when Daddy appeared in the door frame. The hall was dark as I had shut the door to the kitchen to keep the warmth inside, and Daddy was illuminated only by the stars and by the golden light of a lantern he was holding aloft with his right hand.

'Going out?' Daddy asked.

'Just to see where you'd got to.'

'Where's your sister?'

He did not wait for an answer but called her name. The carols stopped abruptly and she came out into the hall.

'Both of you come with me,' said Daddy.

Cathy slipped her feet into her boots before hopping over to the coat hooks and wrapping herself in woollens, rounded off with her navy-blue mack. We followed Daddy out into the cold, shutting the front door firmly behind us. His deep footprints led from the edge of the copse and we followed them back exactly so as not to disturb more of the snow. The ash and the hazel were bare and shivered against the wind each time it blew. Their branches were frosted and held a delicate collection of snowflakes. The hazel particularly, which had been coppiced many years ago, had many surfaces and alcoves in which snow could collect and sit, compacting into itself and freezing anew. Icicles dripped from many of the higher branches where the snow had met the midday sun and slowly melted and found a gradual path towards the earth before being caught for a second time by the cold.

We arrived at the treeline and continued to walk. Daddy's lantern swung in his hand as we bumbled along, and the spindly shadows cast by bare deciduous branches swung and bounced too. When we passed evergreen pines the shadows became furry as the light gathered and parted their needles like water soaking into a dog's coat.

Then the light began to change, and the spindly shadows turned to point towards us, sent by a light that appeared straight ahead, through the trees, growing stronger than Daddy's lantern with every step. The light became brighter but still its source was not clear, obscured on all sides by the trunks of trees and the thick woodland vegetation, blanketed by snow. Indeed, the light reflected off the snow in such a way that as we got closer everything looked bright.

We rounded a huge pine and saw where the light had been coming from. Another pine, much smaller, not much more than a sapling, smaller than Daddy, was covered with lanterns. I looked more closely and saw that each lantern had been fashioned from a milk bottle with a wire hoop tightly wound beneath the bottle's lip and another bent upwards to catch onto the fronds of the tree. Each bottle had oil in its bottom quarter, with a thin metal covering over the top, through which a thick wick poked. The coverings stopped all the oil catching fire at once, but allowed a little to seep up the wick and burn at its tip. The upper three quarters of each bottle-lantern allowed air to move around the flame, and each glowed rich amber, while the light from their fellows allowed the bottles' oil to glimmer too, dancing and refracting as the oil slowly swirled to follow the current up the wick and to the flame, as slow as still water shifting with the earth's tilt. It was a beautiful spectacle.

We stayed out there for half an hour or so, watching the lanterns, playing with sparklers, smoking and chatting, breathing in the cool woodland air. When we walked back to the house we did so in silence, having already got out all our words for the day. I was especially snug in my bed that night. The blankets were warm and close in contrast with the biting open outside. I pulled them up to my nose and went to sleep with that warmth and the scent of worn linen in my nostrils.

Christmas morning came with a bright, white light and left with a slurry of sleet. The landscape had shone with snow and the sky had been glossy. By noon everything was matte.

We roasted and ate the goose and Cathy played her violin.

We went out to the Christmas Tree again that night, and the next night, and every night after that until the twelfth was up, just as Daddy had said. He refilled and relit the lanterns before we got there so the image we saw was identical each time. The grove smelt of paraffin and pine needles rising with the hot air. Timid popping and fizzing emanated from the burning oil.

When Daddy finally pulled the milk bottles down off the branches, he put them in a crate and stored them with his tools. He told us we would get them out again next year, along with the paper decorations I had made. But a few days later Cathy and I spotted that there was also a pile of charred branches and singed needles in the woodpile. They were from our Christmas Tree. In parts they were still fresh, and where they had been cut the soft, greenwood was still visible. But in other places they were black through, and dry and brittle, and with the delicate fronds still coming off some. Oversized charcoal quills. The heat over time had singed them, and some were so burnt it must have been from a lantern whose metal divider had failed and which had burnt all its oil at once.

We went into the copse to see the damage. Again, the greenwood was laid bare where it had been cut. There was no black here, no charcoal. That had all been removed. But the tree looked sparse. It had been wounded – not just wounded, mutilated. It now looked so unlike any of its peers.

We worked wood all the time. We cut boughs and felled whole trees. We burnt it in our stove and hacked it into useful shapes and scrap. There was no reason this should be any different.

Chapter Six

Mr Price was the sort of man who accelerated his car when pedestrians crossed the road. You could hear his engine tighten, raise its pitch, quicken.

Cathy said he liked to see us run but that it was not playful, like when nice men flirt with little kids. Like when kids kick a ball onto the footpath and a nice man keeps hold of it, pretends not to give it back, makes the kids squeal a bit, but then of course does give it back with a wink and a nod. Cathy said Mr Price did it to people he did not like, and to us particularly because he hated us, and because he enjoyed seeing us have to skip the last few steps to safety before his car caught us. She said that he probably wanted to kill us, but got a thrill from the almost, almost, not quite, and besides, he could not kill us while Daddy was around, she said, so instead, he made us run.

Mr Price had a few cars but drove his blue Peugeot saloon when visiting tenants. The ones who paid in cash. The rest did informal work for him on his land or elsewhere. They paid their rents through this work. He preferred it that way. That way he did not have to organise wages and they were his to run like dogs.

For the most part he had inherited the land he owned. Most of the houses in the villages nearby were his and he held the largest acreage of any of the local farmers. Later, he had bought up houses on the estates further into town. These were old council properties. Those that had been bought by tenants in the 1980s as part of the Right to Buy scheme but that were then bought by Mr Price after their owners fell on hard times. The occupants remained but they paid rent again. This time to Price. And this time in cash or in kind.

Mr Price had two sons: Tom and Charlie. They played cricket and rugby at a boarding school miles to the south and lived with their father in the holidays.

We heard stories from people in the village. Stories of two handsome, slick lads who smashed up bars for fun in the knowledge that their father could pay for the damage. Two handsome lads who, when they were still boys, had driven a farmer's tractor through the wall of his own barn and out the other side, slicing a new tunnel clean through the hay. They had learnt a collection of manners at school, though. Now they were nearly men they drove their father's sports cars through the village and, late at night, if they had drunk too much, they rode their quad bikes over their neighbours' crops. Two handsome, slick lads.

Mr Price left us alone for our first summer and autumn in the house but in the new year he made himself known to us. He came to our house from time to time even though we were not his tenants. Daddy had claimed the land, they said, not bought it, and we had built our house here like a fortress.

The first time Mr Price came up he was not in his blue Peugeot but his Land Rover. It was the largest vehicle he owned and we heard its tracks coming up the newly worn dirt road to our house. We heard the dampened popping and cracking of small stones under its implacable tyres. Daddy had been drying dishes at the draining board and went to the window. Daddy's eyesight was good and he had known Mr Price from before but still he did not immediately recognise the driver. He draped the tea towel over his hefty left shoulder and headed out the front door. It was so rare for somebody to come to our house, let alone drive here, that Cathy and I followed Daddy outside.

It was late January and there were clouds of snow-drops on the hillside beneath us. Mr Price parked his Land Rover and glanced up at us as he stepped down from the high chassis. He wore a brown waxed jacket and olive, knee-high wellington boots. His hair was a light grey with strands of white. It was cropped neatly and he was clean shaven. He was handsome and healthy, possibly just less than six feet tall.

For all his brutality, Daddy liked other people. He liked people with as much affection as a huntsman had for his prey, deeply and earnestly but with cold regard. He had few friends and saw them scarcely but the people whose worth he felt were held like rare souvenirs. He took care of those people.

Mr Price was not a man who Daddy liked. He saw who it was. He stopped, stood his ground, and waited.

Mr Price approached and offered Daddy a hand. Mr Price's skin was lightly tanned, stiff and waxy like treated pine. He wore no rings but a gold watch.

'You've given me no warning,' said Daddy.

'I have no telephone number for you, John. How was I supposed to give you warning?' Mr Price took a cloth cap from his inside pocket, smoothed his hair with one stroke from his other hand, and placed it on his head.

'You could've got word to me through someone in village.'

Mr Price shrugged.

78

'Maybe you knew I'd turn you away,' said Daddy.

'I'm sure you wouldn't have turned me away, John. We go back a long way, you and I. I thought you'd greet me like an old friend.' Mr Price smiled. 'And besides, we certainly had something very real in common once.' He now laughed. He had cut glass teeth and scarlet gums.

'What do you want?' said Daddy.

'Nothing much. Or nothing much for you. To me it's important as I'm sure you'll understand.' He looked round at me, then Cathy, then back to me. 'Do you still fly pigeons, John? Do you still keep a loft?'

'No,' said Daddy. 'I hant for years.' Daddy was standing at his full, majestic height. When he pulled the air around into his cavernous lungs he looked lighter than he was, like a circus tent caught in an updraft.

Mr Price pressed him, 'Only I've lost a bird, you see. One of my best racers. Or I thought he was going to be. He's young and I was testing him. He came from the best stock and I had – I have – high hopes. But he should have been back by now. He should have been back in my loft yesterday.'

'Perhaps he's not as good as you thought he were.'

'No, no. I released him not too far away. Over the distance I set him, if he were slow he would have been hours, minutes late. Not a day.'

'Then he's lost.'

Mr Price chewed his lower lip from the inside. 'That is clear to me. I would like to find out why. Has he been distracted? Has he been shot?'

'And this is all you want to talk to me about?'

'Yes, of course. What else?'

'Well I'll tell you plainly that I don't know where your pigeon is. You'll have to ask elsewhere.'

Mr Price had not finished. He shifted his weight onto the other foot and continued.

'You hunt around here, don't you, John? And probably poach a little too, but what's that between friends? Nobody much cares about that around here – there's not enough money in the shooting. And besides, most of the farmers would see it as payment for all the pests you clear off their crops. A pheasant here and there for culling twenty rabbits, eh? Nobody minds that. And you're well known.' He stopped, possibly waiting for a response. When none came he went on. 'But you eat the pests, don't you? It's not just for sport with you. I'd probably discover that these children were fairly nifty at skinning animals. And plucking birds too, I'd say.'

'We dindt catch your bird and eat it. I know difference between a wood pigeon and a racing pigeon. Your bird were got by a hawk and I'm sure you worked that out first thing this morning before deciding to drive up here to my house.'

It seemed as if Mr Price would disagree, but he

did not. After a moment's pause he said, 'I know you're right. I know it. I just wondered if you had seen anything. He was a beautiful bird, you know? I've been working on the line for a decade and he seemed like the best I'd ever come up with. But no matter. A hawk got him and so I'll set some traps and make sure there are fewer around. Shoot any hawk you see, yes?'

'I won't.'

'No, of course you won't. Well, never mind. Let's see how fast his brothers and sisters are, shall we? Let's see if they can outfly the hawks.'

He was about to leave – he very nearly went – and then he didn't. He saw my sister and I again and stopped. 'Your children must be lonely away from school and anybody of their own age. It's just the three of you. They must get lonely.' And then, 'I'll bring my boys up one time so they can make some friends.'

Daddy said nothing. Mr Price grimaced at Cathy and climbed back into his Land Rover. The car curled towards us before taking the track back down to the main road. Its engine was quiet and it disappeared quickly.

Daddy remained fixed to his position for some time after the Land Rover rolled away but his breathing had changed, like a sail buoyed and loosened by an irregular wind.

81

'Why did he really come here, Daddy?' Cathy asked.

She had grown taller over the winter but it had made her weaker. Her bones had stretched and thinned and her muscles had spread to cover them. She could not control her movements as minutely as she had previously. Her knees did not know the length of her femurs and tibias, and her feet smacked the ground when she walked. When she stood up she had taken to resting her weight on one leg or the other with her free foot upended on its toes behind her, tucked behind the supporting ankle. It might have been her hips that had changed. She never would get those wide, birthing hip bones that she feared she would, the ones that conform a woman's whole body around them, but she did get something. Her pelvis developed tilted. Her silhouette took a different line and the small of her back had to curve to meet it before rising sharply as it had done before.

'Where do you know him from, Daddy?' she asked when she got no reply.

Sometimes it was as if Daddy was torn apart by our questions. He wanted to be an honest man who shared what he knew with his children, imparting details of his current and former lives, knowing that if any of the details were too much for us that was the very reason for imparting them. Everything he did now was to toughen us up against something unseen. He wanted to strengthen us against the dark things in the world. The more we knew of it, the better we would be prepared. And yet there was nothing of the world in our lives, only stories of it. We had been taken out of our school and our home-town to live with Daddy in a small copse. We had no friends and hardly any neighbours. We obtained a form of education from a woman who dropped books lazily into our laps from a library she had developed to suit only her tastes and her own way of thinking. She probably resented our presence. She probably thought we were filthy and stupid but gave us her time out of some obligation to Daddy.

That was why anybody did anything for us, it seemed. Around here anyway. They feared him or they owed him favours. Other people did not seem to possess the kind of love he had nor the care he took of them from inside our hilltop watchtower. Others saw reciprocity and debts, imagined threats founded in nothing more than his physical presence, burdens passed onto their shoulders by his existence in their landscape, his insistence on integrity, the old-world morality over which he presided. The lurcher puppies that Peter had given us were tokens of fealty, and while Daddy saw them as complete payment for a service he had really done to satisfy his own frustrations, I knew that Peter still felt the debt, or feared the debt. And it was all because he remained unknown. Daddy could never draw a person in with his temperament. There was nothing generous or reassuring in his manner. The only thing that was known of Daddy was that he was the strongest man anyone had ever met, and that he was ruthless in a fight.

Daddy, of course, knew nothing of this. He could not see into other people's minds any more than he could understand their bodies, so much smaller and weaker than his own. And he could not see any way in which Cathy and I might live our lives without him. We were not built like him and so how were we to stand against the world as he did? He had seen violence, and saw violence now, and he could not understand how a person was to defend themselves or form their place in the world but with their bare muscles and bare hands. And so he kept us here. And I see now that he tied us to everything he valued and feared.

He did not answer Cathy.

Daddy once told us that battles were only ever fought between two people at any one time. There might be armies and governments and ideologies, but in any given moment there was just one person and another person, one about to kill and one about to be killed. The other men and women who were with you or against you faded away. It was just you and another standing in a muddy field with your skin naked beneath your clothes. And Daddy told us that when we met people we had to remember that, to remember that you can only look directly into one person's pair of eyes at any given time.

Cathy asked again how we knew Mr Price, and still Daddy did not answer.

'We must be cautious of Mr Price,' he said, at last. That was all he said.

Cathy stayed quiet. She had folded her arms about her body.

'Will he come back?' Cathy asked.

'Yes.'

Chapter Seven

Cathy and I went to Vivien's house on weekdays. Daddy walked us down and drank hot tea with Vivien, then left us until lunchtime. She gave us lessons like we would have had at school only without the routine that would have been expected there. The lessons were centred on Vivien's interests at that time or the thoughts she was having on that particular day.

Cathy did not keep her promise for long, though she tried. She sat down with the books and papers and made a go of it and joined in when Vivien and I discussed what we had read. But after a while she became restless. She looked out of the living room window into the garden and the fields beyond and even when she was not looking outside I knew that was where her thoughts lay. I tried to speak to her but the words bounced and echoed as if they were leaving the house and disappearing through her into the world beyond. I had an inside sort of head. She had an outside sort of head.

Following her initial efforts, in all but the coldest and wettest weather, Cathy went outside into Vivien's garden. Sometimes she took the book Vivien had given her. Usually she did not. She slipped into the garden then ran into the fields and only came back at the end of the morning in time for Daddy's return and we would all have lunch together as if we had been sitting side by side for the last four hours. Vivien did not stop Cathy nor did she mention her absence to Daddy. And Daddy did not ask us questions about what we had learnt. These were separate worlds.

I preferred to stay in the house. With Daddy and Cathy I spent so much of my time in the outdoors that it was a welcome change. Vivien kept her fire well stoked. When it rained the water ran slowly in thick drops down her double-glazed windows and after a time left a small trail of their minuscule residue. She kept soft blankets folded neatly by her armchairs and cushions that her grandmother and great aunts had embroidered with harvest scenes. Those mornings at Vivien's were comfortable and safe. It was a different life.

Cathy had talked about Vivien's awkward body

but when this woman moved about her house it did not seem awkward at all. Not to me. She seemed unconcerned by the features upon which Cathy fixated. She walked with disinterest. She situated herself effortlessly within her surroundings. Violence did not define Vivien, like it did Daddy. I think this is what alarmed Cathy. I too found it remarkable. I loved my father and my sister but Vivien was not like them. She talked to me about history and poetry and her travels around France and Italy and about art. I began to see a world that suited me in a different way. I came to prefer the inside to the outside, the armchair, the blankets and cushions, the tea and the teacakes, the curtains and the polished brass, and Vivien's books, and the comfort of it all. And while I sat and read and drank tea, Cathy walked or ran through the fields and woods and, in her own way, she read the world too.

On a Monday morning in January, we walked to Vivien's as usual and, as usual, Cathy picked up the work she was given and took it outside. I chose an armchair by the fireplace and wrapped myself in one of the soft quilts. I rested my feet on a small leather pouf the colour of leaf litter. Vivien crouched by the hearth. The fire was unlit. She took old newspapers from the pile and scrunched them into tight balls then packed them into the grate. I watched her place coals on the newspapers then lay strips of wood around the top like the spokes of a wheel. She lit four matches and placed them by corners of the paper such that the body of the structure was slowly overtaken by rippling flames: bright in parts like ice, dull in others like scorched tarmac.

Back at school, I had learnt to read and write and count and add up but when I remembered the lessons it was not the development of these skills but the series of profound revelations that held their clarity. People used to live in caves with woolly mammoths. There were tiny forgotten creatures buried deep inside rocks. There was once a precious little baby named Jesus. Salt and sugar dissolved in water, and this meant they were soluble. Pipistrelles were the smallest bats and they could see with their ears. Rivers cut deep paths through mountains. The moon had no light of its own. Joseph wore a technicoloured dreamcoat.

The lessons with Vivien were different. Today I was supposed to be reading a book about acroplane mechanics. It contained illustrations of the components and diagrams of how they fitted together. It set out American planes alongside their Soviet counterparts and made comparisons between them. A few weeks ago Vivien had told me that she was concerned that she was not teaching us enough about science. Science and technology, she had said. And the natural world. So she had started giving us the books she had about vintage cars, the flora and fauna of the Brecon Beacons, mushrooms and fungi of the British Isles, geology of the Grand Canyon, and the manuals from cameras that had been taken to junk shops years before, with instructions about shutter speeds and aperture settings. And with all these she supplied a dictionary. She wanted to teach us the words in the books, the definitions of the objects and organisms and how to identify them by name. I did not learn much about how anything worked, or why, or how all the birds and beetles stayed alive. I just learnt their taxonomy.

Vivien remained by the fire to watch it take hold. She stretched out her hands to warm them. Her palms turned a light tawny, slowly, from the heat and glow they reflected. I wondered about her taxonomy. I wondered how Vivien could be described.

'What do you do, Vivien?'

'Nothing,' she said.

She stopped speaking and I did not want to prompt her further, but she soon started again. 'Nothing at the moment, but I've done various things over the years. I'm older than you might think.'

I really had no idea how old she might be. My only real comparison for adult age was Daddy, who was so worn yet so vital that it was impossible for strangers to discern his years.

'I've been a painter,' she went on, 'and a poet.

And I've worked in offices for money. And I spent four months becoming a lawyer but gave it up. And I even nearly became a naval officer, once, but that was actually completely ridiculous because I'm not very active and I don't know anything about boats and I've never spent much time near the sea. I mean, I rented a cottage overlooking the Norfolk coast once, but I found I hardly ever looked out of the window, and when I went out for walks I went inland. Strange that, isn't it?'

'When Cathy and I lived with our Granny Morley, we walked by sea all time.'

Vivien smiled without teeth. 'Most people would. But I don't have any real interest in anything, you know. I don't really care about anything. Not about the sea or the outdoors or nature or anything. I don't really have any hobbies. My mother and grandmother used to sew things.' She picked up one of the embroidered cushions. 'But it doesn't interest me. I do things for a bit and then get bored. Like painting or writing. It interested me for a while but I gave up.'

Some sparks flew from the fire and she swept them up and moved away from the hearth. Her knees cracked as they were flexed.

'I think about swimming but I don't swim,' she said. 'I imagine what it would be like to be in the water, especially the sea. I imagine what it would be like to dip my body into the freezing salt water and how it would feel to be fully submerged and then come up for air but I never do it. I don't go to the beach and I don't get into the water. Sometimes I think I could have been an actor. It's the one profession I've never tried. In one way or another, I have spent my whole life impersonating other people. Acting out fantasies with personalities that I've made up in my head. Brave people that go about the world and do things. But it's not like it's the achievements that matter to me, it's the interest. The interest the people I play take in the world around them. I suppose they love it in a way that I don't. They're fanatics.'

She sat down on the sofa but remained erect rather than sinking back into its curves. 'What are you, Daniel?'

'I don't know.'

'What are your father and sister?'

'I don't know.'

'Well if you don't, then how can I? But I do know they're fanatics. When they care about something, whatever it is, they care about it to the full. They care about it as much as anyone can. They don't pretend, like an actor would. They're not concerned with being seen to be doing something. They just do it.'

'Daddy likes to fight,' I said.

'Yes, I know,' said Vivien. 'I know all about that.' She looked as if she did. She looked as if she knew more than I did. I wondered again how she and

92

Daddy knew each other. Daddy the brute and this well-dressed, mild-mannered lady who liked to sit inside her stylish house with her stylish possessions.

'It's his job,' I said. 'He says it's just something he does to get paid.'

'Do you believe it's just a job?'

I looked up at Vivien for a moment. Then into the fire.

'A lot of men feel like they should be violent,' said Vivien. 'They grow up seeing a violent life as something to aspire to. They don't have any real sense of what it means and they hate every minute of it. Your father is not like that. There is a tension about him when he approaches a violent act and a calm about him when it is finished. The times at which he is on edge are those just before he strikes. He is most frustrated when a fight is a couple of months behind him and a couple of months ahead of him. That's when you'll see him shake. Your Daddy needs it. The violence. I wouldn't say he enjoys it, even, but he needs it. It quenches him.' She sat and looked at me. Minutes passed, possibly, but I did not respond and she did not speak again until she asked, 'Have you ever seen a whale, Daniel?'

I told her that I had not in real life, only on the television.

'On the television have you seen a whale breach?' she asked. 'That's when it jumps clean out of the water

93

only to smack down onto the surface of the sea. Have you seen that? The almighty splash it makes?'

I told her that I had.

'We don't fully understand why whales do that but there have been many suggestions. Some people say that it's to see the world and especially the sea from a different perspective, to catch a glimpse of what it is they spend their lives swimming around in. It's like us humans sending rockets up to the moon only to spend the next fifty years gazing at the pictures of our own earth. The whales want an experience like that. A different view. Some people have suggested that it's not a visual experience they're after but a sensual one. When they breach the water they feel the full size and heaviness of their own bodies in the air. They feel gravity and dry cold and when they smack the hard brine with their full airborne weight they quake to their blubber. People say that they're trying to brush off dead skin, barnacles, lichen, and that breaching is like a horse scratching its rump against rough tree bark. But it meets at the same point, doesn't it? The need for a physical sensation that they can't get any other way. That sensation becomes a fixation and each time after they feel it the pressure slowly builds until they can feel it again. I think it's something like that for the whales. They swim around for days, weeks even, feeding and sleeping and breathing and they start to think about that last time they jumped clean out of the water and how it felt when their head, then their body and fins, and then their tail, all emerged from the sea, and how it felt to momentarily hover in a substance that fills their lungs but dries their eyes, and then they remember especially about how it felt to return to the water after their moment in the air. That thump. That splash. The whale continues to think about the breach, more and more, until the urge to repeat becomes irresistible and it erupts out of the ocean only to fall again into it. And so it's sated for a while. Your Daddy's like that, I think. Like one of the great whales. And when he fights it's like one of their breaches. But bloodier, much bloodier. And it isn't a lone act. It's not just an animal and the elements. There's another animal too. Another human. But it's the same. It quenches him.'

Vivien and I spent the rest of the morning speaking of softer subjects and baking cakes iced with buttercream. She kept horses in the large field behind her house and there were always chores to interrupt our routine. We paused from our work to go out and feed them and to muck out the stable.

My sister returned from her rovings before noon. Her mood was sweeter than usual. She smiled broadly as she knocked the dirt off her boots and left them on the slate by the back door. Her face was hot red from the cold and dry from the chill of the wind. Her eyes were alert.

Vivien watched Cathy come in then returned to her task. She did not ask the girl where she had been or why. We were setting the table for lunch and Vivien handed Cathy the bone-handled cutlery to lay around the place-mats as if she had just come down from an upstairs bedroom. Cathy put the items in parallel sets and Vivien went to the cabinet to pull out the plates and napkins. I busied myself at the sink. I washed and dried the tall glasses that had been in the basin since the night before and placed them on the table next to a full jug of water.

'Your father said he was going to bring us lamb chops from the butcher.'

'From butcher called Andrew Ramsey?' asked Cathy.

'That's him.'

'Andrew Ramsey sometimes gives us cuts of meat for no money. They're friends, him and Daddy.'

'They must be.'

'Daddy goes down to village to drink with Andrew Ramsey. He's one of the only men Daddy will drink with.'

'He must trust him.'

'Daddy helped him with some business a while

back. Andrew Ramsey had some trouble with a supplier and Daddy sorted it.'

'He's good like that, your father.'

Cathy nodded. Vivien went back to the kitchen to peel the potatoes and carrots. The chops would not take long to cook. She asked Cathy for help. Usually I did the kitchen work but Cathy was cheerful today and had started a conversation all on her own. They discussed the few people we all knew. Vivien told Cathy that her hair was looking lovely now that it was a little longer and she spoke about how tall she had become. Cathy told Vivien that even if she kept growing, I – her younger brother – would be bigger than her soon. Vivien looked round at me and smiled. I smiled back.

By the time Daddy came with the lamb chops the vegetables were peeled and cut and placed in pans of water resting on the hob. Vivien flicked on the gas beneath them and flames rose against their black-ened bottoms. The chops were wrapped in a blue and white plastic bag. Vivien picked up a frying pan from the draining board and placed it onto the gas, wiping a knob of butter against its rim. She did all this with one smooth motion. Daddy stood beside her and pulled the meat from its wrappings. His hold was gentle so as not to spill the blood that had collected in the folds. They were Barnsley chops. A better cut. He eased the flopping maroon flesh into the pan and the fat hissed and cracked. Jess and Becky came up to his side and stuck their noses in the air and flared their nostrils to catch the savoury steam rising off the meat. I called them out of the kitchen and they did my bidding. They knew that if they did well now they might get scraps later.

Daddy and Vivien stood side by side in front of the hot stove. He was so much larger than her. The ribbed woollen jumper he was wearing accentuated the difference. The lamb was turned in the pan and when it was cooked through Daddy took each piece out with a fork and put it on a board to rest. The second two chops took less time. The pan was hotter and Daddy and Vivien preferred their meat bloody. When the carrots and potatoes were ready to drain Vivien took a colander from a low drawer and placed it in the sink. She poured the contents of each pan into it and then back into the empty pan and onto the stove for a few seconds to dry. The vegetables were then put into separate serving dishes with more butter and Cathy took them to the table.

We ate slowly and Daddy talked to us about Andrew Ramsey's new abattoir. And then he talked about the boiler in Cybil Hawley's bungalow that had exploded overnight. The barrel had split clean in two. Daddy had never seen anything like it. Hot water had come pouring through the house while she was sleeping in her bed and it was a mercy that her bedroom was on the opposite side of the house otherwise she might have been boiled alive. Daddy had cleaned the place up for Cybil as best he could then set her up in the spare bedroom of a neighbour. She was friendly with her neighbours. Most had been born in that street and had lived along it all their lives.

'You take care of people and it always comes good in end,' said Daddy.

Daddy did take care of people. He spent his mornings in the villages around or at the farms of tenant farmers. He had many stories like this.

After we had eaten and cleared away the dishes we left. Daddy walked ahead with our dogs, Jess and Becky, while Cathy and I scuffed our feet behind. The grass up to the house was damp. It must have rained while I was sitting in Vivien's armchair talking to her as she stoked the fire. I thought about the things she had said, about Daddy and the whales, and about violence. The smooth soles of my shoes slipped with each step and more than once I had to put a hand out to steady myself.

We arrived home and Daddy went straight out into the woods with his tools. The shell of our house was sealed tight against the winter but the insides remained rough. Daddy was working on the lining and the floors. Wood was the material he used as much as he could. It was right there in the copse. Trees of different ages and different kinds.

He had a roughly built workshop and storehouse out there, sheltered by the copse so the thin walls and roof did not have to hold too well against the sudden winds that came up over the crest. He kept his tools in the house, to be safe, but took them out there to work on the wood he had collected and felled and sorted into stacks depending on type. Today he was working on walnut for a floor in the kitchen. He said it would last. He wanted everything in the house to last. Cathy and I had been given instructions to clear, clean and smooth the floor beneath so he could lay the wooden planks that afternoon. I had asked Daddy if Vivien could come up for dinner, as a way of thanking her for lunch today and all the other lunches, and the lessons, and, secretly, because I wanted to talk with her again. Daddy said that she preferred to see us in her own house and that she would only come here rarely. He said she liked the indoors and the quiet of her own home and that she was stuck in her ways.

While Daddy was out in the copse, Cathy and I moved the table and chairs and other pieces of furniture into Daddy's bedroom, then got down on our hands and knees to work on the floor. It was hard work. Our muscles soon ached. We scrubbed and smoothed and scrubbed and smoothed but regularly had to stop and stretch like we were getting out of bed in the morning.

As the sun set I pressed my hands onto the cold surface of the kitchen floor and pushed myself up to my feet. I picked the cheese board off the marble counter in the back pantry and carried it through to the kitchen. I spotted Daddy coming from the copse and went to the door to let him in. He smiled broadly at me and took off his gloves and coat and placed them on a chair in the hall. As soon as he had shaken off his boots, his Goliath arms pulled me into an embrace and I wondered what it would be like to touch a real whale, and knew that despite what Vivien had said, Daddy was both more vicious and more kind than any leviathan of the ocean. He was a human, and the gamut upon which his inner life trilled ranged from the translucent surface to beyond the deepest crevice of any sea. His music pitched above the hearing of hounds and below the trembling of trees.

After our dinner, Cathy and I trimmed Daddy's hair and beard as we did every few weeks. He stripped to his white cotton vest and revealed deep scars on his broad shoulders and thick black hair on his chest. He knelt on the floor by a tin bucket filled with water that Cathy had heated. We stretched to reach his head. His daughter stood in front of him with a pair of kitchen scissors and a comb which she pressed against his cheeks and chin. She pulled at the coarse strands and knots in his beard but he did not flinch. She measured the lengths approximately with the comb and snipped and brushed then doused his face with the steaming water to wash away the specks of trimmed black hair. I stood behind and cut away damp locks. Inch by inch they met the keen blades and cascaded. As the jettisoned hairs fell through my fingers to gather around my feet, I softly brushed my knuckles against the back of my father's neck. His skin was smooth there. As smooth as my soft inner arms or the insides of my thighs. He was sensitive to my touch. His whole body quivered and as it did I thought again of the whales. Their hides were sensitive like this despite their size. They were reactive and finely tuned. They could be tickled and teased and just a small human hand on a whale's flank could cause the beast's entire body to ripple in the waves.

After our Daddy was pruned Cathy and I set down our scissors and passed a hairbrush back and forth to draw across our father's scalp and chin. As we did so he closed his eyes and tilted back his head. The beads of water on his face and hair glistened in the crude light from an oil lamp that sat upon the kitchen table and a kind of halo emerged around him as he relaxed each muscle in his body save those in his cheeks that tempted a satisfied smile from his plumped lips. I selected and unfolded a towel from the pile we aired near the stove and rubbed the crisp fabric against Daddy's wet skin. He moaned with sedate pleasure.

III

I stop at a roadside cafe. The windows are thick with filth. Smog from the motorway has caught on the panes and spread like a fungus or a grimy frost. The road licks at the glass with an acid tongue. Plumes from a militant buddleia edge the car park and the cratered tarmac upon which the cars and lorries rest.

I push at the door. It sticks on the frayed linoleum but eases then opens. The sight of people is strange. I am filled with a kind of dread. But the scent of the oil and the frying meat and eggs and bread, and of steak and kidney puddings and mushy peas and chips cooking in dripping pulls me in.

I have not eaten well these last few weeks. Scraps from bins, berries from the verge, raw turnips from a farmer's field. I ate a pizza that had been left out by the railway then spent the next day curled beneath a viaduct cramping and vomiting.

I have come to beg for hot food. I have come to beg for thick custard poured over apple cobbler. I want gravy over Yorkshire pudding. Bangers and mash.

People sit at tables. The sort with the chairs attached. Most are men and most are alone. Lorry drivers hunch over fry ups and magazines. An old lady in the corner is doing a word search puzzle. There is a family with small children at a table by the window. The children are picking at their baked beans and potato waffles. The mother and father grimace as they sip hot coffee. They are neat and tidy in appearance and delicate in their manners. They are out of place here and their eyes shift from each other to the people sitting about and to the servers behind the counter wiping greasy hands on greasy aprons.

'What can I get you, love?' The woman at the till has spotted me from the other side of the room. Her hair is wrapped in netting and a large part of her face is obscured by spectacles. She is wearing catering whites and her hands are placed firmly on the counter before her as if she is holding down the lid of a jack-in-the-box.

A couple of heads turn towards me. Most do not.

I walk down the thin aisle between the tables. I want
to be closer to the woman before I reply so I do not
have to shout over the onlookers. I want to whisper.

It has been weeks since I have used my voice. I
will be hoarse.

The woman smiles despite my filthy clothes and
face. A good sign. She must get all sorts in here.

'Hello,' I say to her. 'I wonder if I could have
something hot to eat. Anything. I handt eaten owt
hot in days. Only I've no money to pay. I'm sorry.
I'm not trying to be funny.'

She makes no sign of recognition. I said the words
so quietly that I wonder if she has not heard.

She nods her head and her smile becomes that of
sympathy. She turns to the girl behind her who
cannot be more than seventeen and has blonde hair
ripped into a tight bun. The woman speaks quietly
to the girl so none of the customers hear. 'Get this
lad a plate of pie, yeah? Whichever we've got most
of. And put a good helping of chips and veg on as
well. I'm not putting it through till so you'll have
to go into kitchen and tell them.'

The girl looks me up and down then does as she
is told.

The woman smiles sympathetically again. 'Take
a seat, love,' she says. 'I'll bring you a pot of tea.'

The tea is well stewed. I mix in the milk and gulp
it while it is still hot. The plate is brought. Meat

and gravy pie with more gravy poured on the top.
The peas and carrots are coated too. The plate steams
and brings bitter evaporated Bisto granules to my
nostrils. Chips on the side. I sprinkle salt and vinegar.

So much food.

The generosity of strangers.

Some strangers.

The out-of-place family get up to leave. They
fumble for change and place some silver coins on
the laminate table top. The little girl picks her nose.
The boy takes hold of his mother's hand. The door
swings shut behind them.

I devour my meal. I look around to see if I am
watched before licking the plate clean. I am brought
hot apple crumble and custard and consume them
as hastily as the pie. I lick the bowl. I take my plate
and bowl and teapot and teacup and saucer and
cutlery to the counter. I thank them all and thank
them again and they smile and nod.

The kindness of strangers. The kindness of
women. Women who share cakes with neighbours
and volunteer their time with the local PTA. Women
who listen. Women who talk.

I leave the cafe. The car park is bright and the
surge of traffic is close and tight.

A lorry driver leans against his cab. He watches
me then speaks.

'Need a lift?'

Chapter Eight

Our mother lived with us back in the house with Granny Morley. At times. Now and then. She came and went. Like Daddy. Sometimes she would bring herself to our door, sometimes she would be brought. Sometimes we saw her before she went upstairs to her room. Sometimes we did not.

When she was at home she slept. It was as if she was a thousand years old and each of her days lasted a month. She would get up, get out of bed, and leave. Then she would return weeks later as if she were coming home from work or from a day out. Then she would sleep through her night while we came and went, got up and went to school, had lunches and dinners, went to bed.

When she arrived I washed her clothes. When she left I washed her sheets.

Her clothes she placed in a bag outside the door of her bedroom. Granny Morley would send me up to get it. I would bring it down to the utility room beyond the kitchen, which was always cold and damp. The cold and the damp rose from the worn linoleum floor and I would have to sit with my feet up against the gas fire for hours afterwards to feel dry again. The cold and damp soaked through my socks to my feet and up my legs to my body and head. So did the warmth when I sat at the fire.

I would empty my mother's washing onto the floor, loosing the drawstring of the bag, turning it upside down and shaking it out with each bottom corner clasped between a thumb and forefinger. Tops, socks, knickers, bras, a pair of jeans. A small collection, carelessly strewn. There was carelessness too in the way the garments had been kept. The socks were well-worn at the heels and at the toes bobbles had appeared. Elastic had become detached from the small pairs of knickers, cut from synthetic fabric designed to imitate lace. There were more tallies than the lace-like fabric had intended and these were frayed. Whites were grey now and greys were lilac. Blacks that had been the colour of the night sky now had the smudged, matte finish of a rubbed chalkboard.

The jeans were worn at the knees and the crotch. Mainly polyester with elastane and a small amount of true, cotton denim, the jeans had stretched and retracted many times but now they had come to follow the contours of my mother's legs and hips.

She was thin. Always so thin. The clothes had little definition but from them I knew her body. I knew the colour of her long hair, strands of which had fallen among the laundry. I knew the smell of her skin. I knew these things much better from the clothes than I ever did from seeing her, touching her, listening to her.

With Granny Morley I would sort the washing by type and put it into the machine in separate loads with the powder and the fabric softener. I would close the door and turn the dial and press buttons that commanded the water.

Granny Morley and I drank cups of tea while my mother slept upstairs, for as long as she needed to sleep.

At the ends of her visits, the bed sheets were left outside, then she left too. Wet with sweat, wet with blood. Always twisted and pulled, the evidence of a writhing body. And the smell of her. On the sheets and in the room when I went to clean it. Bitter smoke and salted sweat, and sour spit and the sweet iron of her blood. The scents reached out to me and lingered on the tip of my tongue and at the back of my nose and throat. The memory of smells and tastes and faint anguished bleats from behind the closed door of her room.

I once asked Granny Morley why we found my mother's blood on the white sheets. She replied that my mother bled when she was broken.

The last time she came to the house there was no more fuss than on any of the other times. She said no more to us and we said no more to her. She behaved no differently. Daddy had been away too but he came back after a phone call from Granny Morley and lay in the bed by my mother for days, holding her, whispering to her gently. I heard them from outside the door, but caught none of the details. And I think Daddy was taken by surprise more than any of us when she left. She had seemed healthier, brighter, for the few days before but then slipped off, like she always did, with no goodbyes. Daddy was startled. Me and Cathy, we expected it, and Granny Morley too, I think. But Daddy was startled. He looked for her. But Granny Morley got a phone call and when she put down the receiver she turned to us and told us that our mother would not be coming back.

Chapter Nine

Mr Price returned to our house two weeks later. This time he brought his sons. Tom and Charlie Price were both tall and slender. They had long, thin legs and narrow torsos that gave way to wide shoulders so abruptly there was clear daylight between their ribcages and upper arms. Tom was older and had dark blonde hair, cut around his ears at the front and shorter at the back. Charlie had dark hair and darker eyes that were very unlike his father's or brother's, and although he was strikingly handsome there were greyish semi-circles bleeding from his lower eyelids. He had a hooked nose and skin that took on the colour of the day. This day was overcast so his skin was fragmentary and pale. They all wore green wellington boots and waxed jackets.

The Price men ascended the hill in their Land Rover. Cathy and I were sat a long way behind the house amongst the outlying trees. I was whittling green ash. I had stripped the tender bark from a piece the length of my hand span and was turning it and rounding it with a squat blade. Cathy held the corpse of a mallard between her knees and was pulling fistfuls of feathers from its dappled skin. A bowl of steaming water and a pile of wet rags lay at her feet for her to dip them then dab them, hot and sopping, onto the bird's supple pores.

We did not see or hear them knock at the front door. Mr Price went into the kitchen to speak with Daddy. Tom and Charlie came to find us. They laughed candidly at private jokes as they walked through the still-green bluebell shoots.

These boys were just so handsome. They were so much more handsome than me and Daddy, we could not even be compared. We were almost distinct breeds, adapted to different environments, clinging to opposite sides of the cliff. It was as if Daddy and I had sprouted from a clot of mud and splintered roots and they had oozed from pure minerals in crystalline sequence.

They spoke and laughed with deep voices that were not like Daddy's. They were smoother, though muted with vocal fry. The sound resonated against the cool air like a ball bouncing on wet grass.

'Did you shoot that bird?' Tom asked me. He was talking about the duck that Cathy was plucking but he addressed his question to me rather than my sister.

'No,' I said. 'Daddy did.'

'Daddy?' He seemed amused by the word.

'Yeah,' I said, simply. 'But it wandt on your land he shot it.'

I did not know why I had said it. Daddy might have shot it on Mr Price's land or he might have shot it elsewhere. I had no idea but saying it meant Price's son thought that we were guilty of something or else knew that it was something we sometimes did. I should have known better but because I had stumbled and because he had remained silent in response, I went on again: 'He dindt shoot it anywhere near your land.'

'Well if he shot it anywhere around here then he shot it near our land. He would have had to go very far away for it not to have been near our land.' Tom paused to laugh at my absurd scrambling. 'Do you hunt with him ever?' Tom asked.

'Only sometimes.'

'He's got a twelve-gauge shotgun, hasn't he?'

Cathy looked up at Tom but neither of the boys turned to her.

'I don't know,' I said. 'He might have one but we've never seen it, and he doendt hunt with it.'

113

'That's odd that he'd have it and not shoot game with it. How does he hunt?'

I shrugged. Daddy had traps set up throughout our copse and in the fields around. They were not the sort that killed the animal they snared but those that kept it waiting until Daddy came to collect it and kill it himself. It was better that way. Traps that try to kill the animal usually fail and the poor thing lies there dying slowly until it is finished off. The traps that our Daddy used lured the animal with a trail of food then shut it away in a box. There was room enough in the box for comfort in its last hours and the animal had no sense of its fate. Daddy checked the traps regularly and if he found something he would take it in his hands as quietly as he could then snap its fragile neck. The little creatures never even knew they were dead.

Sometimes he fished. Daddy had rods and tackle but said that fishing with rods took too much time and that it was better to tickle the trout. He knew the places for that.

I told the lads that I had never known Daddy to use a shotgun but that he hunted game with his bow.

'Rubbish,' said Tom. 'Nobody hunts with bows around here. I don't believe that anyone's ever been able to shoot a bird with one. Not a bird in flight.'

Cathy placed the half-plucked mallard on a cut section of tarpaulin on the ground by her feet and

114

squeezed her hand into her right jeans pocket to pull out her leather tobacco pouch. She pinched at the dried fibres and placed what she pulled onto a folded paper. She stuck a filter at the tip before rolling it between her fingers and licking then sticking the seal. She lit the cigarette with a well-struck match then sucked on it such that the flame dimmed to glowing ash and smoke seeped from her nose and mouth. She watched the lads.

I shrugged again. 'Daddy does. Sometimes Cathy does as well.'

'Is that Cathy over there?' asked Tom. She was sitting no more than five metres from him but he asked me about her without turning in her direction. For a moment, Cathy continued puffing on her rolly. Then she got up and walked over. She had grown in the last couple of months and had become ungainly in her gait, unused to the new lengths and angles of her limbs. She was upright in everything else that she did, though. She always had a certain direction.

'I hunt too,' she said. 'I've shot birds like this bird with my bow.'

Tom turned to her and as he did he became angry. Surprisingly so, considering how small the disagreement should have been. Probably no one ever spoke back to him. Not his little brother nor anybody at his school nor the boys he played rugby and cricket with nor the men in his shooting club, not even his teachers. They were probably too taken with him. Him and his confidence. Him and his arrogance. That charm that he walked around in like a swarm of horseflies about his head. Nobody probably ever told him that he was wrong. Nor would they ever, it seemed. For his whole life. He would always get his way. Always be right. Always get to bat first. I doubted even his dad questioned him much, even his own father, Mr Price. And then on the occasions that he did they both knew that they were upholding the proper order of things. When his father asked him to explain himself, or rethink something, or when he questioned him or told him that he – Tom – was incorrect, it served to strengthen Tom's position, as second only in the universe, to be first when the time came. In those moments his father was putting Tom Price in his place but that never constituted a slight.

But with Cathy talking back at him, when he had not even been talking to her in the first place, well, it must have been frustrating. I could see it in his face. He clenched his jaw and blinked rapidly, as if trying to blink her away or blink away the thoughts he was being forced to have now that his train of conversation had been minutely offset. 'I just brought it up because it seems odd – counter-intuitive even – that your father hunts with bows and arrows when he could be hunting with a gun. Regardless of whether or not he does have a twelve-gauge shotgun lying around, he could just get one, couldn't he? Or some other kind of gun? I don't understand this predilection for old technology. What's the point?'

'Well what's the point of any of this?' said Cathy. 'We could just live in a town and Daddy could get a job and we could buy all our food in a supermarket like everyone else does. And go to school and have friends, and that. I mean, you might ask why we don't just do that?'

Tom laughed. And I knew it had been coming. 'You're right, I could just ask that. Why are you living here in the middle of our wood?'

Cathy had opened her mouth but the other son, Charlie, quiet until this point, stepped in. 'Tom,' he said, 'we don't need to get into that. Don't be an idiot.'

Tom looked startled at his brother's intervention but said nothing to him and nothing more to Cathy. He again turned away from her and directed his comments to me. He asked about the copse. He asked about the trees within it, the types and the ages. He asked where we had lived before we came here. He asked why Daddy had chosen this spot. He asked how long it had taken Daddy to clear the land and to build the house. He asked about our mother. He asked whether we went to school. He asked how long we would be staying.

I did my best to evade the questions and, after a time, he became frustrated.

'I'm just curious about your lives, that's all. You must admit that it's unusual, you lot living here. And in the way that you do.'

I looked about myself. Cathy had returned to the bird. She took it again in nimble hands, her plucking more resolute. She tore at the creature with the quiet fanaticism of a flagellant at his own skin but though her fists pulled at the downy fluff with pressing haste, she did not draw blood nor did she damage the flesh. She doused it with the water, though it had cooled, and wiped off the stubble and residue that marred the otherwise pristine carcass.

I answered the tall, smart lad as best I could. 'Daddy thinks it's important we learn to live with things we ourselves can make and find. That's all. We just want to be left alone.'

'You mean you don't want to be friends with me and Charlie? Did you hear that, Charlie?'

Charlie appeared more reticent than his brother. More thoughtful, perhaps. 'Yeah,' he said. 'That's a shame.'

Tom looked at his brother for a moment then over at Cathy then at me. He had become bored by the conversation and wanted to get moving. He suggested we return to the house where their father was speaking with our father. Tom and Charlie walked that way and I thought it best to follow. Cathy too. The plucked bird swung by her side: plump and bobbing.

We followed the tall lads into the kitchen. The inside heat was thick. Daddy and Mr Price sat facing each other on opposite sides of the scrubbed kitchen table. We hovered around the edge of the room but the men concluded their business and both pushed back their chairs with a searing scrape against the floor. They stood to their full heights. Daddy was a giant. He towered over Mr Price by at least a foot but the smaller man did not cower.

Mr Price held out his right hand. 'I hope you will think about what I have said, John.'

At first Daddy held back, both arms fixed tightly to his sides, but then he released one to meet Mr Price's. His expression remained blank.

The visitors directed themselves out of the house then down the slope towards their Land Rover. Daddy leaned against the murky kitchen window to see the vehicle leave. He watched it all the way down the track, round the corner and along the bottom road until it was out of sight.

He placed his right hand in his left and massaged his knuckles. They were rigid from fractures and calcification and there was barely any flexibility in the rough, taut skin that wrapped them let alone between the joints. He rubbed the thumb of his left hand across the many, composite scars, feeling almost nothing in either hand, his nerves having receded after repeated bruising. He performed the action for memory and motion rather than sensation.

We stared at the lost man, our father, partly blind to us as his body grasped itself and he slipped again into his own thoughts, alone in his motion.

He returned to us in due course. 'Put another log in the stove, Daniel. I want for us to be warm again.'

I slid into the hall where the dogs were sat in their straw bed. They jumped up at the sight of me and sniffed and licked my hand as I lowered it to stroke them. I placed my palm on Becky's head and she lifted her muzzle so as to catch me above my wrist and bring the hand down into the reach of her tongue. I wrapped my hand around the other side of her head and she lifted her muzzle again so my outstretched arm and her jaw danced round and around in circles.

I broke free and stepped over the dogs to get a log from the corner behind their bed. I returned to the kitchen with both pups at my heels and closed the door behind them. They leapt and sniffed at Daddy and Cathy and I busied myself at the stove while Daddy continued to talk.

'Do you know why I built our house here?' asked Daddy.

I looked at Cathy. She hesitated. 'We thought you

must have bought the land from the travellers or else won it in a fight.'

'I dindt buy land,' answered Daddy. 'I dindt win it in a fight neither. As far as Price is concerned we don't own it, not in the way he sees ownership, at any rate.' He shifted in his seat. 'Your mother lived round here. When she fell on hard times, Price seized a lot of what she had. But when your Granny Morley died it seemed like the right place to come, to build a home, to live as a family. Because of your mother. And because I knew we would care for this land in a way Mr Price never could, and never would. Mr Price does nothing with these woods. He doendt work them. He doendt coppice them. He doendt know the trees. He doendt know the birds and animals that live here. Yet there is a piece of paper that says this land belongs to him.'

Daddy raised himself from the chair and paced over to the stove where I was finishing stoking the fire with the new log. I poked it and shunted the dead embers into the grate.

'Does Mr Price want us to leave our home?' asked Cathy.

'He does and he doendt. He coundt give a stuff about these woods. But he's taken us moving here as a hostile act. He thinks I'm trying to provoke him. Perhaps I am. But regardless, he's made it clear he'll cause as much bother for us as he can. There were once a time when I worked for that man. When he used my muscles to bully weak and poor, to make sure they paid their debts. I were useful to him, and he wants me to be useful to him again. But I won't. I won't work for any man ever again. My body is my own. It is all I own.'

Daddy took the poker from my hands and thrust it into the heart of the fire where it stuck into the fresh log which lay atop the flames but was barely touched by their flickering edges. He twisted the iron rod and rent apart the grain and split the log into two frayed sections whose frills caught easily and transmitted the fire to the wood proper. The glass door of the stove flashed as he shut it.

'He'll start by causing small nuisances for us that'll build and build until they become unbearable. He'll make sure people in villages begin to freeze us out. They'll stop serving us in shops and stop speaking to us. That won't matter much. We hardly buy owt and we hardly speak to anyone either but it'll be an inconvenience. That's how it begins. Then he might send people round when we're out to silt up our well and we'd have to bore a new one. After that we'd always make sure that someone was here. We'd be afraid to leave. And so in that way he would have begun to control our movements. Then he'd have bricks and dead rats thrown through our windows, and dog shit left by our front door. Then they'd start picking on you two when you're out alone.'

'We'd be a match for them,' Cathy interjected.

Daddy shook his head. 'I'm sure you would be at first,' he said. 'When you have the advantage of surprise on your side. That'll always be your advantage, Cathy. Nobody will ever expect you to fight back and certainly not in the way I know you can. But once they've realised you're no pushover they'll send more men and those men will be tougher and nastier and even you won't be a match for them all.'

'You would be though,' said Cathy assuredly.

Daddy shook his head again. 'I win fights because I am suited to the rules of those fights, Cathy. They're a test of strength and speed and endurance and I am the strongest, fastest and toughest man in Britain and Ireland. But take away those rules and it's anyone's guess who'd win. If someone pulled a knife on me, or a gun, well I've dealt with those things before, I don't mind telling you, but that doendt mean I could again. It all depends on circumstances. And if it's one against many then, well, the odds are stacked. And that's not to say I woundt try. You two know me well enough. But I have to be realistic.'

I took for myself a thick slice of brown bread from the board and scooped butter from the churn to slide across it. The dogs watched me with begging brown eyes and twitching black noses as I bit and tore and chewed. I pondered my father's words. I watched my sister as she sat with that duck corpse on her lap and hunched her shoulders against the glum news. Daddy placed both his hands flat on the table, his bowed fingers and knuckles almost camouflaged against the likewise knotted, ecru oak.

I sat and turned towards the warm stove. 'What shall we do?'

'Price's hope would be that I'd do his work or that we'd move away.'

'This is our home,' I said.

Daddy looked at me as if for the first time in weeks and he placed his right hand on my left shoulder. 'My feelings are the same,' he said.

We stayed together in the kitchen for the rest of the afternoon. We drank mugs of hot, milky tea and at around four o'clock Cathy pulled a couple of bottles of cider from the cupboard. We discussed what Mr Price had said to Daddy and what could be done. Daddy told us again that Mr Price cared nothing for the copse. Daddy said that Mr Price just hated to feel the weight of helplessness. To interfere with the lives of others was to carve for himself a presence in the world. Mr Price detested that which he could not control. We lived here on his doorstep yet he had no access to our lives. We did not pay him rent, we did not work for him, we did not owe him any favours. And so he feared us. Daddy said that to Mr Price people were like wasps zipping around his head, ready to sting at any moment. He liked to know their movements. He liked to know their intentions. And when he knew those things he could catch them and put them in a breathless jar.

Daddy said that we should seek out his few friends in the village. There were a handful of people that he had helped in recent months and though Daddy was reticent in his favours, there were perhaps a couple he felt he could confide in. His friend Peter had less affection for Mr Price than we did and we resolved to pay him a visit.

Chapter Ten

We went the next evening. The morning we spent together on the rough, wet grass outside our wooden house. After an early start Daddy carried the kitchen table and chairs outside and set it up with a chequered cloth. I got the eggs and bacon on. Cathy brewed the tea and we took it all outside to eat in the cold bright sun. The bacon was from the butcher, Andrew, who was also one of Daddy's few friends. It was well salted and he had cut it thickly but I made sure the rind was crisp before I lifted it from the skillet. The eggs fried quickly in the bacon fat and took on salt from the meat so their bottoms formed caramel crusts while the yolks remained golden. I warmed the plates first in the oven before serving up and afterwards finished them with a slice of fresh bread.

Eating a full breakfast outside with my Daddy and sister was always a joy but this morning more than ever. There were troubles, we knew. Our home was in danger. But right now, with a bright white sun shedding its light onto my pale, thin arms, and thick crispy bacon held between two slices of soft, warm bread, I could not have been happier.

A clutch of gulls cut through the eggshell sky, their bellies caught in dark shadow.

Breakfast and its lazy aftermath took most of the morning and the afternoon was spent in the copse or round about. We set and checked traps and Cathy and I called Daddy to make the kill if there was a catch. Otherwise we saw to the hens or cultivated the kitchen garden as it was needed.

Daddy contacted Peter in advance from a pay phone in the village. We walked down together as dusk fell and Cathy and I huddled outside while Daddy went into the box with a stack of ten pence pieces. The spot stank of piss.

It had been an old, red phone box but the paint was chipping and now it was little more than a rusted metal shell. The glass in its panes was cracked but not yet smashed. Daddy picked up the receiver and I heard an amplified crunch and its echo then a clear dial tone.

Cathy pulled out her smoking equipment and started to roll up. The ground was already strewn with cigarette butts of various ages like little brown slugs slithering in different directions through the ash-stained mud. She rolled a cigarette for me too and lit it with a match from a box in her top jacket pocket before turning the match to the end of the roll-up she was holding between her lips. I inhaled as deeply as was comfortable and blew my smoke in the direction of my sister and up into the night air.

Daddy's voice sounded muffled from within the box. He spoke to Peter briefly and gave him a few details. When the conversation finished he pushed open the door, took the cigarette from my mouth, took a drag and replaced it.

'Let's go.'

It was half a mile walk but we hardly spoke along the way. The main street through the village was lit with amber streetlights. Security bulbs flashed on from the houses by the road as we passed. They darkened again almost as quickly. Some of the houses had televisions playing that could be seen flickering behind the closed curtains. We passed a house where a man and woman were shouting at each other and a baby was crying. Daddy slowed as we passed that house and listened hard but then walked on with us and the shouting and crying faded to nothing.

Peter's house was on the outskirts of the village and had a long back garden that stretched way out amongst the fields. The house itself was not much bigger than ours. 1970s build. Pebble dash. The inside was sparsely decorated. A TV stand but no TV. CDs but no hi-fi. That sort of thing.

His bed had been moved into the back room so he no longer had to climb the stairs. The double doors through to there were partly open and revealed a jumble of sheets and pillows and a couple of green beer bottles and a box of tissues on the bedside table.

'So Price wants you to work for him?' said Peter as soon as Daddy, Cathy and I had sat down. 'He'll be getting you to kick me out of here, next.'

'You're his tenant?' asked Daddy.

'I am,' said Peter. 'At least I have been so far only I can't afford the rent any more. He wants me out, faster than even law would get me out. I bet he'll want you to do it. Break you in by getting you to shift a friend from his home. He'll know you helped me that time. That time you saw to Coxswain in that car park.'

That evening we drank the best part of two bottles of whisky. Daddy said the day merited something hard and sent Cathy out with a well-used fifty pound note to get the best spirit stocked by the village shop. Daddy and Peter drank the lion's share between them. They poured approximate double measures into their glasses then returned for more.

Cathy and I drank more slowly and mixed our whisky with drops of water. She smoked and I had a few too. We stayed in the men's conversation for the most part but dipped out now and then.

'Most people round here rent their houses from Mr Price,' said Peter. 'And if they don't rent from Mr Price, their landlord is a friend of his. All the landlords round here go drinking and shooting up at manor. They all have dealings, as they say. They'll have money invested together. Bubbling around in the same pot.'

'Where's pot?'

'I don't know, John. Don't ask me. I don't even have a bank account any more and when I did it's not like I had cause to care much for interest rates and investments. But they all have fingers in the same pies. All landlords round here. All led by Price. They've all got investments in same businesses and give each other tips. Trading tips. Farming tips. Landlording tips. That sort of thing, I don't know. But Price is top dog. Always that. So if he takes against someone, they're out. And it means that – one way or another – Price owns county.'

'A lot of his business is legal then?'

'Most of it. Ninety per cent of what he does is above board. It's just you see other ten per cent because that's world you're in, John.' Peter let out a half-laugh. 'Why? You thinking of following some kind of paper trail? Uncovering evidence? Going to police?'

Daddy looked at his huge, knotted hands. 'No. No, you know I could never do owt like that.' He almost blushed. 'And you know I could never involve police, neither. As you say, what's ten per cent of Price's world is all of mine, as well you know. Nothing I have is based in any law.' He looked over at Cathy and me, watching him gently. 'Not land. Not cash under my bed. Not my profession. Not even them.' He nodded at us. 'Not even my children. I don't know if any law or piece of paper could connect them to me. But they're mine through and through, that's plain to see.' He looked back towards Peter and drained his glass. 'And I woundt involve police anyway. They belong to Price around here too. Big ones anyway. Police chiefs and councillors that I've seen driving up to manor.'

Peter refilled Daddy's glass and continued to speak. 'I know of two familics he's put out on their arses in last year because they coundt meet rent increase. But don't take my word for it. You'll need to speak to others if you want to know more. Ewart Royce and his wife, Martha. Ewart's the cleverest man for miles around and he still cares about area. He were a union man, back when the pit were still open. And he were a decent one. He's well connected among the people who aren't connected to Price. Ex-miners, sons of ex-miners, tenants, labourers and unemployed. He knows about the law too, though I know you don't want that. But he's part of your world too. He likes a bet. He likes a horse-race. He likes to watch a good fight and he trades with travellers and gypsies as well as working men. You want to know how to keep your house? You should talk to Ewart Royce.'

We stayed up for hours. Daddy and Peter drank all through the night and I fell asleep in the beanbag I had been sitting in with my head propped against a cushion that was in turn squashed between the radiator and a cabinet. I woke thirsty and when the first light came up on the horizon I went to the sink to fill my empty glass with water. I drained it and filled it for a second time to take back with me to my makeshift cot.

Peter was asleep in his bed and Daddy was there too, under a thin blanket, sprawled with his head at Peter's feet. Cathy had made herself as comfortable as she could on the floor with cushions, a duvet and her head resting awkwardly on the other beanbag. I saw an empty glass by her left hand. I picked it up, rinsed it under the tap and filled it with water for when she woke up, parched like I had been, and needed a drink. She stirred when I placed the full glass on the floor but not enough to wake. I returned to my place by the radiator, shut my eyes and slept intermittently for the next two or three hours.

Daddy, Peter and Cathy woke only when the sun was so high in the sky it could not be ignored. It was nearly 10 o'clock and it was bright. Sharp rays had nudged the hems of the thin poly-mix curtains to the sides and filled the room with a precise light.

Daddy rolled to his side, woke, and was up. He headed straight to the bathroom. I heard the taps running and the sink filling with water and a few minutes later the sound of that cold water being displaced by his head as he plunged it beneath the surface. The door opened with his elbow against it, pushing. He had taken off his shirt and had washed his body too. The black hair on his chest was wet and soapy where he had not rinsed himself properly. He was rubbing his face dry with a tea towel but water dripped from his hair and beard onto his shoulders and onto the carpeted floor below. He roughly shook out his shirt and put it back on, fastening the buttons from bottom to top.

Peter stirred. He was slower to wake than Daddy. Cathy was lying on her back. Her position was the same as it had been when she slept but her eyes were now wide. She watched Daddy as he buttoned his shirt. I had been sitting up on my beanbag for some time, sipping water, unable to sleep but unsure of how to be awake.

We left the house soon after. A girl, a boy, two men. Hungover, half-asleep. We stopped for a quick breakfast at a bakery on the High Street. In the mornings it served bacon, sausage and egg sandwiches. I had bacon then asked Daddy if I could have an iced bun like a shy child with a sweet tooth. He paid 50p for three. For the road, he said.

The Royces lived in a nicer part of the village where the houses were well-spaced and the gardens greener. There were cars here, parked in driveways, washed and polished. The privet hedges were trimmed regularly and the well-mown front lawns that sat to the sides of the gravel drives were surrounded by planters, ready for the spring shoots. Net curtains obscured every window and most were so clean and clear it was as if the glass was hardly there.

The Royces lived in a house with double-glazed windows. They drove a dark blue Volvo. There was an undersized fountain in their front garden that was half-hidden by an overgrown buddleia. The water burbled from within a shard of limestone.

Cathy, Daddy and I waited by the gate while Peter offered himself to the front door. It was only fair to give them warning, Daddy had said. Like with Peter.

The wheels of Peter's chair negotiated the gravel easily and he shifted himself with his strong arms onto the step to reach the bell. A woman came to the door first and looked down at Peter while he spoke to her in a voice I could not make out. She was smaller than me. Possibly 5'4". Her hair still had some dark blonde but it might have been dyed. This made her look younger than fifty but something else told me she was older. It was not that her face looked old. It was not that her neck looked old, though it is the neck which tells the greater truths. She did not have wrinkles or rivets that I could see from my place by the gate and her skin neither drooped nor darkened in places where brown spots of age might come to appear. If these were there she had hidden them well. It was the way she held her body that told me she was in her late sixties. It was the way she planted her feet on the floor and the way she sat her hips and the way she held her shoulders. The woman wore baby pink tapered trousers that were fastened over a plump waist. She positioned a jumper fashioned in sweatshirt fabric covered with printed, photo-realistic flowers at the waistband. Cream, fluffy half-slippers covered her little feet. Gold rings adorned her hands and there was gold too at her ears and at her neck. She wore large, plastic, purple, oval glasses that covered her face from her cheeks to her eyebrows.

A man approached. He lifted his right arm up behind the woman to lean on the door frame. He wore olive-green trousers that were so dark they were almost brown and with a sharp crease down the front of each leg. He wore a white shirt under a maroon V-neck jumper but no tie. He spoke to Peter and listened to his wife then looked over at Daddy and then at me and at Cathy. He beckoned us inside.

The vestibule was cramped as we all gathered in it to take off our shoes and our jackets and to place them in the cupboard or hang them on the coat stand. The carpet was soft with a pink and gold baroque pattern like the pattern on the carpet in Granny Morley's entrance hall years ago and miles away. The walls were cluttered with pictures in varnished wooden frames. Most were photographs of children in school uniforms against a cloudy lilac backdrop. The children appeared to have been grouped in sets of siblings, either two or three together. The same children had been photographed at different ages, their hair lengthened and shortened. At some point, each had been photographed with missing front teeth. There were too many children (and all given equal precedence) for these to belong to the Royces. They were nephews and nieces, godchildren, the children of friends and friendly neighbours.

Peter made the introductions briefly when we were

in the vestibule but he had given a fuller account of whom we were while we had waited by the gate.

Martha invited us to come through to the lounge. She was primarily speaking to Cathy and me. Ewart was already leading Daddy through.

Martha asked us if we wanted tea or coffee. I asked for coffee. Martha left the hallway and bustled into the kitchen. I heard the kettle being lifted from its stand and filled with water. Cathy made for the sitting room and took one of a couple of chairs by a table in the corner. Daddy and Ewart sat on the large, satin armchairs that took pride of place in the room. Peter wheeled his chair around and back into a position between the two other men, to the side of the fireplace. There was an electric fire on the hearth that had not yet been lit that morning.

Martha returned from the kitchen with a tray of mugs, a bowl of sugar and a milk bottle. The liquid was hot and bitter and I poured in as much milk as the vessel would take and stirred it with three teaspoons of granulated sugar. It went down easily that way and the cup was soon half empty. I could drink coffee and tea when it was still piping hot unlike Cathy who always had to wait for the liquid to cool. It was the only thing I could best her at and so of course I turned it into a competition and made a show of it when I could. Once, years ago when we still lived with Granny Morley by the coast, she had become so angry at my skill that she had swallowed the whole cupful in great, scolding gulps, almost as soon as the water was out of the kettle. She had burnt her mouth and her tongue and even her throat and the blisters had lasted for over a week. She had done it to show me she could, but had soon learnt her lesson. Even I could not down hot drinks that quickly.

It was the same with the cold. I could bite hard into scooped ice-cream and I would bare my teeth to do it to show my sister that I could. I could swallow ice-cubes whole. In the winter I would take handfuls of snow and stuff it into my mouth or rub it onto my face or body in front of her. She would pour ice and snow down the back of my jacket, right under my jumper and shirt, and I would stand motionless like it had not affected me at all, like I could not even feel it. It would drive her mad. She would shiver even from the touch of the snow against her gloved hand as she picked it up to do the deed. She would shiver from even that and there I stood, still and smiling, like I was having my morning shower. It made her mad.

'He's a slimy toad,' said Martha as she came back into the room with her own cup of tea and took a seat on the edge of a footstool. 'He always has been, and I've known him for a while. Not well, mind — I'd be surprised if he even knew our names — but

I've known him from a distance. Everyone around here has done, or those of us who've been around a while and still have our memories. As a young man he were always sloping around where he wandt wanted. He were a little thing, then. He'd suddenly turn up on his better-than-yours bike and start causing mischief. He'd make sure he'd get his own way and if he dindt that's when the threats would start. His father had quite a force of labourers then, before everything was just one man and a tractor, and even then if any of these men wanted to keep their jobs – casual work it was – they'd better do what young Price told them. Farm labourers, day labourers, seasonal workers dindt have unions. Not like them lot in pit villages who went down mines. Like my Ewart. Farm workers had to do what they were told and they did. And I reckon there were some pride in it. Doing young Price's bidding and beating up a couple of miners' sons. There were a bit of rivalry there, you know.'

Daddy listened to what Martha told him. He made no movement nor signal of recognition.

'Well, that were when he were a lad. He spent most of his time away at boarding school, of course, being from family he's from. But in summer months, during long holidays, he'd be back round here trying to pick fights with lads. He never had much time for us girls, mind. Not to chat to, anyway. I suppose

most teenage boys are like that but him even more
so. Sometimes he'd have friends from school come
to stay. Never one or two, always a whole gang of
them together, when his father was down in London
or away elsewhere. They'd have manor to themselves.
They were interested in girls then, when they were
all together. And some of them were very charming,
of course. Real posh boys, well-dressed, immacu-
lately groomed, taught how to speak politely up at
that school. And I knew of girls – common, ordinary
girls from round here – that went up to manor with
them. For a chat and some dinner, like. Well I heard
rumours of what had gone on and after a while I
stopped listening. Wandt the type of thing I liked
to hear about. But I caught enough to know kind
of boys they were. And boys like that don't grow
into decent men. Boys who get girls drunk and share
them around like a cut of meat.'

'Safer that way for some boys,' said Ewart. 'They
can look searchingly into each others' eyes rather
than into terrified faces of girls they're holding.'

Ewart placed his tea on the floor by his chair.
Martha picked it up and placed a thin cork coaster
beneath it.

'So he's been making more mischief, has he?' said
Ewart.

'That's right,' said Peter. 'John here would like to
take man down.'

Ewart looked my Daddy up and down, from the bottom of his polished work boots to the top of his furrowed forehead.

'Woundt we all,' he replied. 'But he's not like you or I. He's a different class. He could be taken down by one of his own and he probably has been. Or that's his fear. Ever wondered why he bothers with all of us? Ever wondered why he doendt just take his money and muck about amongst his own sort? Well I have. It's because he can't. He's afraid. So he interferes with our lives.'

They talked for hours about the Price business. Martha told stories that she had gathered from many years of listening. Stories from across the West Riding and beyond. Stories of evictions, disappearances, suspected corruption in the county council. They spoke of how it was to be resolved. Ewart talked about direct action. He spoke of the way things had been when people who lived together in the same communities also worked together, drank together, voted together and went on strike together.

I stopped listening after a while and I know that Cathy did as well. There was a dog-chewed tennis ball beneath the table and Cathy and I amused ourselves by softly kicking it to one another. The trick was to kick it with enough accuracy that it would hit Cathy's feet but lightly enough that it would not bounce away. Then Cathy could retrieve it and roll it into the correct position with the soft sole of her foot and kick it back. Only once did I miss and the ball darted across the room and settled by the radiator beneath the window. Cathy got it back subtly though. The conversation had become so serious that only Daddy noticed the error and he shot his daughter a sly wink.

Revenge. They were speaking of revenge. Revenge against Mr Price and against everything that was invested in him. Lost money that really stood for lost time and lost children that really stood for a kind of immortality, just like Granny Morley had always said.

And then there was Ewart Royce, who had tossed and turned against the slow rot of the decades and against the new order that took him further and further from any kind of future for which he had hoped and imagined and prayed and fought.

When we lived by the coast, Granny Morley had taken us to an old war memorial. It was the sort fashioned in the style of an Anglo-Saxon stone cross with men's names carved onto each of its four sides in order of military rank. Each time we saw the memorial she told us that millions of men had died dancing in the old style. I had not understood. I had puzzled over her meaning for years and only occa-sionally came to attach her words to some new and small piece of knowledge about human nature and the history of the world. Something about the thrall of performance and the retarded values of nations. Something about men who play out the same scenes again and again and who try to remedy all blunders and remove all errors in plot and description. Men who wrestle backwards through the acts.

I half listened to the plans that were being made now in this lounge between my father and these new friends. I could not help but feel that they too were dancing in the old style and appealing to a kind of morality that had not truly existed since those tall stone crosses were placed in the ground, and even then only in dreams, fables and sagas. Only then in the morality of verse.

Chapter Eleven

Spring came in earnest with clouds of pollen and dancing swifts. The little birds, back here to nest after a flight of a million miles, were buffeted by the wind, which blew hot then cold and clipped unripened catkins off the ash. The swifts were too light to charge at the gusts like gulls or crows, and through them I saw wind as sea. Thick, pillowy waves that rolled at earthen, wooded shores and threw tiny creatures at jutting rocks. The swifts surfed and dived and cut through the invisible mass, which to them must have roared and wailed as loudly as any ocean on earth, only to catch the air again on the updraft and rise to the crest. They were experts. They knew how it was done. And they brought the true Spring. Not the Spring that sent timid green shoots through compacted frost-bitten soil but the Spring that came with a rush of colour, a blanket of light, unfurling insects and absent, missed, prodigal birds on this prevailing sou'westerly.

When the heat was up, traveller lads from the caravan site down the way took off their tops and rode their 125cc dirt bikes round the lanes bare-chested. They bezzed up and down with boxes of ferrets clipped to the backs of their bikes and they looked for fields or verges with good networks of warrens. They popped the ferrets down the holes and out they would come again with wriggling rabbits for the lads' suppers.

Cathy liked to watch them. She desired them. She itched to join in but we did not dare to ask. Instead we hid in ditches or behind hedges and scouted them. That became our game. We stalked the lads like they were our prey. We watched them wrestle with the ferrets then with the rabbits. None were as expert as Daddy with handling animals nor at dispatching them quickly and cleanly at the last. There was more blood than there should have been and more kicking and squealing. One of the lads was a big boy with thick ginger hair and a torso that freckled rather than tanned. He got bitten by one of the bunnies and how he howled. He had to let the rabbit go and the poor thing jumped and ducked left then right then back into its hole and out of sight. Blood splashed from its hind legs as it went and I knew it would not last long. It was a shame. It would have done better to have been got by Daddy and to have ended up in one of my pies, I thought, than to be half caught by a lad who has only half learnt how to catch you and then bleed to death slowly over the next few days or else lead a fox right to your warren with the scent of your blood and be devoured along with all your family.

Still, we watched these lads all the same. We watched the habit of their movement and the manner in which they held their bodies and the way they sat on their bikes, slouching easily while their bowed arms stretched to the handlebars and revved the bikes' engines.

We saw other people so rarely we were fascinated by the news that did happen past, and though I loved watching birds and beetles, watching human beings was the thing I loved the best.

After catching the rabbits, the traveller lads got on their motorbikes and kicked back against the dirt then sped along the next lane and the next to find more of what they were after. We could follow the noise for a while but unless they stopped again nearby we could not follow to stalk them any longer and they were lost to us. We waited until the next time they came hunting or the next time they raced their bikes. In the meantime, there were always rabbits to watch.

There was a night I could not sleep even though I had tired myself out working with Daddy in the copse all day. My back ached from swinging a large axe up and around and down onto the logs that Daddy had felled. My forearms ached from wrapping my slender hands around those logs and placing them onto the chopping block, and from thrusting the small hand-axe down onto them with my other hand time after time, to split the wood for burning in our stove. My thighs burnt from squatting and picking up bundles of the stuff though it was too heavy for me, and carrying it to Daddy's store or up to the house. The ground in the copse was rough and strewn with branches and rocks and leaves that had fallen unevenly and rotted hard over seasons. Uneven earth cut apart by the growth and death of thick roots. My calves ached from a day of finding purchase on this unsteady ground, and the skin on my face was sore from the salty sweat that had trickled down from my hairline slowly for the last several hours.

My eyes, however, were as fresh as they had been that morning, and were filled with the dappled light that had shone through the quivering leaves all day,

147

and with the colours of the wood and the image of my father stooping and rising as he felled branches for us to collect. Because my eyes were so bright and alive, my thoughts were too. Each time I reckoned I was falling off into sleep a colourful memory of the day returned and revived me. I skipped between waking and sleeping for the best part of two hours then peeled back the covers of my bed and pulled myself upright. I tucked my feet into my slippers and walked through the two doors to the kitchen.

There I found my sister stood at the window with her right hand raised in front of her face. She held back the curtain so as to look out into the night. The sky was dark but for a thin moon waxing and but for Venus forming a concentration of the sun's rays above the horizon. She loomed larger than I had ever seen her.

A jug of home-made cider sat on the kitchen counter. Cathy had drunk perhaps half.

'You're up too, Danny.' She only called me Danny sometimes. She had heard me step over the threshold and stop to look past her at the night sky.

I told her that I had been unable to sleep and that I guessed she was unable to sleep as well. I suggested that the both of us might just be too awake because of the day of working and because our bodies were tired but our thoughts awake.

'I think I were too angry to sleep,' she said.

Her statement shocked me. I asked her why she was angry.

'I'm angry all time, Danny. Aren't you?'

I told her that I was not. I told her that I was hardly ever angry and then she told me again that she felt angry all the time.

She told me that sometimes she felt like she was breaking apart. She told me that sometimes it was as if she was standing with two feet on the ground but at the very same time part of her was running headlong into a roaring fire.

I stayed up with her for a couple more hours until the jug of cider had gone and we had drunk another one besides.

When she agreed finally to go to bed, I returned to my room and fell asleep so quickly I almost forgot the events of the night. It was as if they had been a dream. A dream of fire. Indeed, in those days I thought that the most prolonged conflict in my life would be the one I faced every night against my dreams. Sometimes I thought I could sleep for ever. Sometimes, pulling myself out of a dream to be awake and alive in the world was like pulling myself out of my own skin and facing the wind and the rain in my own ripped-raw flesh.

Chapter Twelve

'That bastard who won Lottery.'

'Who?'

'That bastard who won Lottery. Euromillions, I think it were. Not main prize, but enough. Already a millionaire and he wins Lottery.'

Cathy and I were in the car park down behind the back of the Working Men's Club. The tarmac must have been forty years old. Winter frosts had cracked through its crust so many times there were more craters than ridges, and large gnarled clumps of the stuff, broken into rough, lithic formations, had been kicked to the sides of the rectangle like gargoyles in the rubble of a fallen cathedral. In patches, the artificial surface had cracked and crumbled so badly that only black earth remained, scorched by the tar. If the car park had once had white lines to mark its bays they had long since vanished. Chewing gum flecked its surface white and grey.

The morning mist hung around our knees. It would not be a cold day but it was cold now, just after dawn, cold and dim, the sun's rays caught in clouds that were bobbing on the horizon.

'Fucking Euromillions.'

This was where men met if they wanted work. There was little to be had around here. The jobs had gone twenty years ago or more. There was just a couple of warehouses where you could get work shifting boxes into vans. At Christmas-time there were more boxes and more vans but still not enough. There were jobs here and there for women: hair-dressing jobs, nannying jobs, shop-assistant jobs, cleaning jobs, teaching-assistant jobs if you had an education. But if you were a man and you wanted odd jobs or seasonal farm work this was where you met. A truck came through and took you off to the fields or more usually to a barn nearby where a combine harvester dropped its load on the floor for sorting: sugar beet for sorting, turnips for sorting. And potatoes. Today it was potatoes and the men knew they would be taken up to Sunrise Farm to work for the bastard farmer who had won the Lottery.

'At least he gives us time off we need to keep signed on,' said one.

'Drives us up there if we're going to miss an appointment.'

'He fucking has to, though. If he keeps us signed on he doendt have to pay us as much. He just slips us a tenner at end of day like it's fucking pocket money.'

'And he'll go and dob you in if you cause a fuss. He'll go and tell job centre you've been working for him and he'll rustle up some bits of paper he says he's been giving you all along. Payslips and legal stuff. Stuff you've never seen before in your life but then it's suddenly there and it's your own fault for claiming benefits and for not paying tax or summat, all in one go. Happened to Johnno.'

'Happened to Tony.'

'Happened to Chris, and all.'

'Bastard.'

'Bastard.'

'Wanker.'

The farmer was a bastard, then. Like most others, they all agreed, but this one particularly because he had won the Lottery when he was already a million-aire. He was a lucky bastard. Euromillions. Or a scratch card.

Cathy and I were like grey standing-stones at the border of their coven. They mainly ignored us. We stood at the edge of the car park, a little way away from their cluster in the middle but close enough to hear. We had brought a flask of hot coffee. I sipped it out of a white and blue enamel mug while Cathy drank from the lid.

Potato-sifting at Sunrise Farm. That was the job today and the van would be here soon to pick us up. Give us a lift. Drop us off. Pick us up again when the day was done. Drop us back here.

Cathy was nervous. I could tell from the way she gripped the flask lid. I could tell from the way her thin and translucent eyelids blinked against the cool air. Her eyes were sensitive like her skin and could not stand the cold. They were especially sensitive when she was scared. When something worried her she kept them wide against it, whatever it was, so as to see it coming at her then to see it off. Today, fear coursed through her like a hare through wheat stubble. I could tell. She bristled.

I was afraid, just the same. Sunrise was farmed by this millionaire lottery-winner and his name was Coxswain. It was the same Coxswain that Daddy had seen to for Peter's money. The money he had been owed. It was Coxswain who Daddy had nearly killed outside the back-room betting shop. Coxswain was one of Price's friends. It was Price's land like all the land around here and Coxswain held it, ran the farm, worked the labourers hard for a tenner a day and dobbed them in to the dole office if they complained.

Cathy and I were here to see what was what. Those were the instructions Daddy had given us. It had been Ewart's suggestion.

We were to look at the farm and chat to some of the workers to find out what we could about Coxswain. If we could discover something about Mr Price, so much the better, though Daddy doubted there would be any chat about him. The men who worked on these farms did not know who owned the land or who managed the managers or what the turnover was like or what proportion of profit got translated into their wages. They sorted the potatoes, got paid and sometimes they went down to the pub or corner-shop and bought a packet of cigarettes.

We had almost finished the flask of coffee when the van arrived. Cathy took my mug away and tossed the dregs aside. She put it into her bag with the flask and our lunchtime sandwiches.

A man with a clipboard and a spongy pewter moustache climbed out of the driver's seat. The men and Cathy and I walked slowly towards him and huddled around. Hands were in pockets and jackets were zipped as far up as they could be zipped. The man made a note of each name before its owner climbed into the back of the van.

The foreman spotted my sister and me. 'What's this?'

Cathy stepped forward, prepared. 'We're here to work. Same as everyone else.'

'How old are you?'

Cathy shrugged. 'Does it matter?' she said.

'I asked, dindt I? How old are you?'

'Eighteen,' she lied. 'And he's sixteen.'

'He's your little boyfriend, is he?' said the man, obtusely.

'Brother.'

'How did you hear about meeting place?'

She shrugged again but the man did not seem too fussed by the rudeness. 'Same as everyone,' she said. 'Someone told us. Someone said go down to WMC of a morning if you want to earn a bit of money. So that's what we did.'

'Who's your dad?'

'Sam Jones. Do you know him?'

It was a common enough name. I was not sure if it was someone she knew of or if she had pulled it from thin air there and then.

'Never heard of him. Do you know any of this lot to vouch for you?' He nodded at the men already sitting in the van and those still standing in the car park.

'We heard you were short of hands this year so we thought we'd come down and try our luck.'

The foreman stopped to consider. He blinked a couple of times. His eyelashes were as grey and as coarse as his moustache. 'That's true enough. We do need some extra. Are you up to it?'

Cathy shrugged.

'It's hard work. Bending and lifting all—'

'Not that hard,' interrupted Cathy. 'We've sorted potatoes before. And picked them. And carried great big sacks of them. It's no problem. We worked on a farm near Grimsby where we did potatoes and sugar beets and all that.'

'Grimsby? What the fuck were you doing over there then and being here now? You a pair of fucking gypos?'

'Our nan lived over there. We used to live with her. Now we live with our dad.'

'Your dad, Sam Jones?'

'Aye.'

He did not believe us but he let us on the bus all the same.

The last of the men in the car park were marshalled onto the van and they found their places among those that were already inside. The seats were coated in a sticky fabric that was pretending to be leather. There were gashes in some and seat-padding was spilling out. Some gashes had been made deliberately. They had been cleanly slashed by a bored and frustrated labourer who had sunk the blade of his penknife into the soft cushion rather than into the taut muscles of his own thigh. Most of the holes were from wear.

The foreman had left the engine running and the radiator on. It was gorgeously warm. The windows had steamed up so the cold world outside looked like it was shrouded in a close fog. I made my mark with my finger. I traced a single line of about six inches across at the height of my eyes like the thin slit in a knight's helmet. I looked out through my visor. My nose pressed on the glass made a further mark in the damp glaze.

The van was not half full and Cathy and I were the only two people sitting next to one another. All of the men had chosen a pair of seats for themselves so they could spread themselves out with an arm up on the neighbouring headrest or their coat or bag between them and the aisle. They all appeared to know each other quite well but they protected their individual space nevertheless.

A man sat in the row directly in front of us. He was wearing a black beanie hat and a bomber jacket that was more British racing green than military green. When the doors were shut and the driver had got going, the man took off his outer clothes. Beneath his hat he had a shaved head and on the back of his neck a tattoo of a word or phrase written in a gothic script so dense I could not make out the letters. Beneath his jacket he wore a white vest. He bore the signs of a thin man who had worked hard to build himself up. His muscles rested uneasily on his bones.

As he arranged himself in his seat he noticed me looking. He turned and used the window as his back-rest so that he could face us and talk.

'Not seen you two before.'

'Needed money,' said Cathy.

'Aye, don't we all.'

He had brought an apple with him and began shining it on his trouser leg like a cricket ball. He then raised it to his mouth and took a bite, cleaving a quarter of the apple's flesh with a loud crack. He chewed what he had bitten off and swallowed the mouthful before turning back to us.

'You must have got desperate if you've come up to work with us lot,' he pointed out.

'Suppose so,' said my sister.

'Not seen either of you before, is all, and it's shit work, this.'

'Is it?' said Cathy. 'How shit?'

'Shit.' He lowered his voice, 'And bosses are right bastards. Us lot only do this work because we've got no other choice.'

'How come?'

'Most of us are just out of prison, or else our working record is so bad we can't get owt official. Dole-wallers, the lot of us. Only bosses encourage it. They drive us up to our probation office or job centre to get our money, and they know that way they can pay us less.'

'How much?'

'Twenty quid for a ten hour day. Cash in hand, mind. The days are getting longer, and all. Hardly anyone wants to do it any more – not even Lithuanians – it's not worth it. It's just us few who'll put up with it. We fancy an extra bit of cash on top of our dole-money for a few pints and a packet of cigarettes.'

'I roll my own.'

'Do you? Clever girl. You got any for me?'

Cathy took out her tobacco and began rolling a cigarette for the man. When she had finished she passed the ivory stick between the headrests of the seats in front and he placed it behind his right ear. 'Can't smoke it now. Will save it for later.'

'Who is boss?' asked Cathy.

'Coxswain today. He's one of worst, but none are good.'

'Who else do you work for?'

'All sorts. All the landowners round here. Sorting potatoes and that, and doing odd jobs. There's casual work in slaughterhouses too. Jim Corvine's a boss. Dave Jeffreys. Price.'

'Price?'

'Aye, Price. He's one who fucking terrifies me, but we don't see him much in person. Too important, that one.'

'Aye but when you do see him, what's he like?'

The man shrugged. 'Like I say, I've not had much

contact with him. None of us have. Only I know not to mess with him. One of lads a couple of years back, maybe it's five years now, got his leg badly mangled in some machinery up at Price's farm. Don't know what work he was doing for him but it was after dark and place wandt lit properly. Well Johnno – that's name of lad – he got talking to some men down pub and next thing I knew he were trying to get some money out of Price. Some compensation for his injuries.'

'Did he succeed?'

'Did he fuck. He got half his family evicted from homes. Price owned lot. Not only was he evicted but also his poor little mum, his sister with her new baby who had a flat up in Donnie, and even a fucking cousin or summat, who lived in a house of Price's right on other side of county. All of them turfed out as quick as you like. You don't fuck with Price, no you do not. Oh yes, there's many of us who'd like to take that man down a peg or two but there's few who'd dare.'

'Would anyone dare?'

The man shrugged and took another, similar sized, bite from his apple. The edges were turning golden brown.

'Someone who's got nowt to lose, I suppose.'

Cathy looked at me. I felt her thigh move closer to mine and we began, unconsciously, to breath in unison, knitting ourselves together in a common cause.

The van was drawing in to the farmyard. There were some shallow outhouses made from red bricks and corrugated iron and a block of stables in the distance. There were two large barns, one of which had been painted blue and the other of which had been painted white but so long ago that the colour was flecked and faded and both barns were now for the most part the colour of metal in rain. The tall doors of the barn had been cast wide open to give the men light in which to work.

The man's name was Gary. He told us as we were getting out of the van to begin the day's labour. We worked close by him for the next ten hours, maybe more. We stopped for a short while for cups of tea and Cathy and I snacked on the lunch we had brought. Gary introduced us to some of the other men and he told them what we had been whispering to him while we worked. He told them that we had a daddy who thought he could bring down Mr Price or at least stand up to him. Some laughed openly and others turned away to conceal their laughter. But not all of them. Some looked me and Cathy up and down as if trying to gauge the measure of our father by sizing up his offspring. If that is what they were doing they were likely to be surprised. I was still a little lad and though Cathy had that great and alarming strength about her, she was still just a girl in their eyes. Gary, at least, seemed convinced by us. He had spoken directly to my sister after all and Cathy was nothing if not compelling. Without fail, her eyes made contact with whomever she was speaking to. She stared, blinking only occasionally, and so quickly and faintly that it could almost be missed. She did not laugh nervously where others might. She committed to her story where others were prone to waiver, and she always believed everything she said – a kind of honesty to which few could admit. There was some hope in her words, I suppose, and Gary was pinned. Through him others were convinced too and Cathy spotted a good moment to invite them up to our house as Daddy had instructed us. They were to come and we would light a bonfire, drink beer and cider, and cook meat on the open flames. A few said they would come there and then and Gary said that he would bring more. Cathy urged him to remain quiet about our business. He assured us he would be canny and I believed him. That evening we passed their names to Ewart.

Chapter Thirteen

Caring for a wood means huge stacks of trimming get piled up around the place. In order to let new growth fight through, overhanging branches, crumbled bark and fallen trees must be cleared. Weeds in the undergrowth must be managed. The right shoots must be let through and the wrong ones discouraged. Hazel needs to be hacked back to the stem so that it sprouts forth again severally next season like the heads of Hydra.

The multiple, thin trunks that come from hazel are useful for building fences and baskets and they form the wattle of wattle and daub walls. Daddy, with our help, had been rebuilding and extending the chicken coop with wattle and daub and something like a thatched roof, though Daddy admitted a proper thatcher would be loath to give his approximation that name.

The new chicken coop was attached to our house. Its back wall was what had been the outside of our kitchen wall, by the stove. This meant the hens could enjoy the warmth that seeped through the wood and stones, such that it did. Daddy said that most people kept their chickens at the bottom of the garden far from the human house so that the human family need not be bothered by the clucking and scratching of the birds. Daddy said this was unkind and that he would rather live with the racket than think of the creatures left needlessly cold when there was a clear and direct remedy. So we built their house tucked up close against ours. Its wattle walls were curved and crinkled like a callous on the smooth, straight lines Daddy had constructed for our home the previous year. A grotesquely large wasps' nest glued to the side of a silver birch.

With all that work for the chickens and all the continuing work to restrain and shape the copse, the piles of woodland debris grew and grew. We burnt much of it in our stove but every now and then we set a load ablaze in an outdoor bonfire. We picked clear evenings for these, even if the cold was biting, and we stood about and warmed ourselves against the baying flames and roasted cuts of meat or vegetables or else we toasted bread as we had when we first arrived and lived out of the two vans.

Now, we had much wood to burn and this time decided to bring others along to our bonfire. We invited Andrew the butcher and Peter and Ewart and Martha, and Gary and the other labourers that Cathy and I had made contact with. Ewart suggested an event to get to know people properly, to foment support or sound out the people and the possibilities that lay in our community. Martha said that we had been alone for too long.

Maybe so. The prospect of so many faces coming up the hill to see us felt strange, like we were to be stripped naked and paraded.

This said, there was excitement as well as fear. I busied myself with arrangements for the food we would serve. I calculated the amount we would need and saw that we got it in the days before. I picked spring vegetables from the patch and chopped them into chunks before setting them on skewers to char over the fire. I picked out some large potatoes from our store. The new potatoes in the ground were too little to disturb so I went to these hefty lates that we had kept dark in hessian sacks from last autumn. The store was running low but the ones I chose would be big enough and I wrapped them in tin foil so we could place them on the embers of the fire. That way they get all smoky as they cook and the skin becomes crisp while the white flesh on the inside melts like hot dollops of cream, not far in texture from the butter we would drizzle over the tops. Daddy sorted most of the meat but I ground offcuts and entrails and made little patties with barley and spice.

We invited Vivien too.

I met with her almost every day. Sometimes she would leave me with reading or work to finish in silence. On other occasions she would stay with me and chat. I cherished these conversations and when I could think of a good one I would ask her a question about what I was reading in the hope that her answer would be long and detailed and that it would lead us to other topics, further questions, new answers.

The thought that she would be coming up to our home excited me. I liked the idea of seeing her in a new place and showing her around the spaces I inhabited with Cathy and Daddy. I wanted to show her the trees in our copse and the chickens and my vegetable patch and the house itself. I wanted the chance to tell her things she might not know. This was my land and I could show it to her. If there was time I wanted to take her up to the railway tracks. There would certainly be trains passing while our guests were with us but I wanted to take Vivien, especially, up for a closer look.

The same old trains still ruffled on past, despite it all. I wondered what the train driver thought, and what the passengers thought, when they looked out the windows as dusk settled and saw our copse, and the crest, and the trail of thin black smoke coming from behind it.

It was set to be a mighty blaze. Daddy had rooted out all the dead wood he could find: dead brambles from the hedgerows, fallen branches from an oak that were obstructing a bridleway. A beech had been struck by lightning in a midsummer storm the year before. Its dead wood had hung limply ever since, festering in the formation in which it had once grown. Daddy pulled the worst of it down and carried it back to ours. In the days before, as I had been making my preparations, he had been breaking up all this wood and vegetation he had collected and going about the process of drying it as best he could. Under bits of it he lit little fires then packed the wet wood on top, as if he were making charcoal.

On the afternoon before the evening Cathy and I helped him move it all to the allotted location. Daddy insisted that we move it for the final time rather than burn it where it stood, in case any little animals had made their homes there. Sure enough, Daddy picked up a big old log and a little hedgehog blinked in amazement against the daylight before rolling itself up into a tight ball and presenting its bristles. Daddy picked up the creature carefully in his massive leathery hands and carried it to safety.

When we lit the construction it was clear there was still a good deal of water amongst the branches, twigs, leaves and logs. Steam came off it in sweeping flurries and it fizzed and popped like a boiling kettle. But the fire took hold and, with attention, soon the flames sent up wreaths of smoke rather than hot steam. The afternoon wind was busy and changeable, swirling one way and then another. This was good for the fire but bad for us. Cathy and I could not work out where to stand and on more than one occasion we ran back from the fire, having been sent into retreat by the billowing black smoke.

By the time the first of our guests arrived, the dancing amber flames reached deep into the dusk. Ewart and Martha Royce came up with a basket of teacakes for toasting and soon afterwards Gary and ten of the other men arrived, to be shortly followed by a dozen more who had also been given the address. A few of the men looked over at Cathy but with Daddy by her side nobody would ever give her any bother. Many had brought girlfriends or wives and a few had brought little babies and kids. Andrew came up from the village and so too did Peter and other people from the villages around whom Daddy had helped out or who had just heard what was going on. Most people brought drinks and some food to cook on the flames, so even though the food I had prepared soon ran low there was more. Nobody went hungry.

As the evening progressed, Ewart Royce gathered men and women close to him, one or two at a time, and spoke at length and directly to each one. He spoke about their livelihoods and their homes. He asked about the work they did and how they were payed. Who owned the house in which they lived. To whom did they pay rent. How much was that rent. Mostly, the men and women answered. When it came to relating the sins of their employers and landlords, most had no compunction. Who could blame them?

A woman in a fleece and jersey tracksuit came forward. Her long, dirty-blonde hair was held in a low ponytail at the nape of her neck. She gripped a lit cigarette between the ring and middle fingers of her left hand and told Ewart about the man who owned her bungalow. 'At least when I paid rent to council, I felt I could get things fixed. It were a slow process, always, but someone would come eventually and see to cooker, or whatever. I knew who to go to. I knew there were some kind of, what's word, process, no matter how tricky. I gave my money to council and I kept place nicely and in return I got a decent place to live. Now it's a private landlord and he doendt give two stuffs. I don't have a fridge any more. The wires went last year and it handt been cold since. It's just another cupboard. That's how I use it, like a cupboard.' Some others laughed. The woman encouraged it, laughing too with a warm guttural giggle. 'Call me naive, but it were only really then I realised it were just land. It were as you were saying to me before, Ewart. The landlord wandt there to provide a service, as he saw it, or to offer owt in return for money I paid him. I were paying him money for land. For right to live on land. This might seem obvious to all of you, but it wandt to me, not when council was my landlord. Then I thought money was for upkeep of house. But, let me tell you, house could come down tomorrow and Jim Corvine would still come for that cash. It's land. Only land. I'm paying to live on a piece of land that we, all of us, used to own together. And I'm working as hard as I ruddy can to get enough money to pay for that land that we, all of us, used to own together. And I can't see reason for any of it, any more.'

There were murmurings of accord.

Later, I saw Ewart standing twenty metres or so from the fire by a table that carried the salads.

'You got everything you need, Ewart?'

'Oh aye. It's a fine spread. You saw to this, did you?'

I nodded.

Ewart helped himself to a spoonful of coleslaw.

He laid it on a floury bap and wrapped up a hunk of just-charred meat.

'A good turn out, too,' he noted. 'You and your sister did well at farm. And Martha's sister, Julie, did well at Post Office. She got word to those in village that pop in for cash pensions and benefits and like and those that draw cash for rents.'

'It's a good crowd,' I agreed. 'Do you think much will come of it?'

'It's hard to say,' said Ewart. 'I don't know folk round here like I used to. I can't tell how they feel any more, or how they think. Sometimes I think spirit's dead and gone, but sometimes I think it's still there, just resting its eyes. A lot of those here are sons and daughters of men that worked with me up at pit. So many passed away before their time. They drank too much and smoked too much and ate too much of this meat. We all did. But I do see something here of that old world. People are as poor now as they ever were, and as tired. And bringing people together of an evening is easier than keeping them apart. And by that same token, bringing a community back together is easier than setting people and families at odds. It's just that that's where all effort's been this last ten years and more.'

Ewart took a bite of the burger and mayonnaise dribbled down his chin. I passed him a napkin from the table and he wiped his face. I saw that Vivien had been standing with us. She looked at Ewart uncertainly. I was not sure if they knew each other but before I made to introduce them, she spoke.

'It wasn't all that wonderful, all the time. Those men who would come together so naturally to support one another would go home drunk and beat their wives.' Ewart was caught for a moment. Vivien continued, 'There are dreams, Ewart, and there are memories. And there are memories of dreams.'

Ewart waited for a moment longer, and then, 'Aye'. The old man nodded and smiled ruefully by way of departure. He walked towards the drinks table, where Martha was busying herself filling plastic cups with cider from a barrel.

'Do you not think it will work, Vivien?' I asked.

She simply shrugged.

Chapter Fourteen

I was at Vivien's house the next day. She sat with me and talked for the best part of the morning but in the afternoon left me alone in front of the spitting fire and climbed the stairs. She had plans to meet a friend in town later that afternoon. She told me she would be staying there in the evening and going to a restaurant in Leeds then the theatre to see a play with this friend and she would stay over with her or him at her or his house. She did not say 'him' or 'her' at any point, though I listened hard for those words, and she did not mention her or his name, though I listened hard for that too. I asked questions that would ordinarily force use of a name or a 'him' or a 'her'. She answered the questions politely, brusquely, but used none of those words.

I heard her moving around in the room above. The floorboards creaked and the heavy oak wardrobe door clicked open and shut. The rap of wire coat-hangers on a steel hanging rail carried clearly. Glass perfume bottles jangled against their neighbours as Vivien nudged the dressing table and pulled drawers from their tressels.

I heard because I listened closely.

I had been upstairs in Vivien's house only once. The downstairs bathroom had been in repair and there had been wet paint on the walls.

My first thought, though I was ashamed to think it, was that upstairs was not quite as tidy as down-stairs. Certainly it was not pristine. There were piles of books on chairs on the landing and an overflowing wastepaper basket. The tightly spun spider plants on the windowsill were tarnished at the tips and the soil in their pots was bone dry. The windows required a damp, soaped cloth on both sides. Greasy fingerprints marked the light switches and door handles.

The vinyl bathroom floor had been covered with a thick, browning rug, flecked with rose-scented talcum powder. I found a tub of this on the shelves behind the toilet. I knew the substance from our years with Granny Morley, when she would lift Cathy and I out of the bath, rub us almost dry with a towel, rub that soft talc like icing sugar onto our skin then help our little legs and arms step and slip into jersey pyjamas.

Above Vivien's bathroom sink was a glass shelf beneath a mirror which held a couple of toothbrushes lying on their sides and a half-squeezed tube of toothpaste, its blue-specked gel oozing.

I had left the bathroom and meant to go straight back downstairs. Vivien had been in the kitchen pouring loose tea into a teapot. The kettle had been in full boil and masked any sounds she made down there or any sounds I made up here.

But the door to her bedroom had been ajar and, in all honesty, I could not help it. I was able to slip through the crack without pushing it any wider.

There was a pile of clothes on a chair in the corner and more on the bed, clean and dirty, and the wardrobe stood open.

First I had gone to the wardrobe and run my fingers down the arm of a silk blouse of dull ivory with fine violet embroidered petals and picked at its chipped mother-of-pearl buttons. Then I had taken a cotton dress on its hanger from the wardrobe and held it up. It was narrow at the waist and wider where the material hugged Vivien's breasts and hips. When she wore dresses or buttoned-up blouses they often struggled to stretch over her breasts. And when she wore skirts they were tighter over her hips and sometimes quite baggy at her slim abdomen.

I was skinny all over. My sitting bones could be seen and felt through my slender, pale buttocks, and I was conscious of it. My chest was thin too. My muscles were underdeveloped and my rib-rack stretched my skin almost translucent, and the edges of the bones were outlined in shadows when light came at them from above.

I had moved to the unsorted laundry on the bed.

You have to appreciate that I never thought of myself as a man. I did not even think of myself as a boy. Of course, if you had asked me I would certainly have replied that that was what I was. It is not as if I had ever actively rejected that designation. I just never thought about it. I had no reason to think about it. I lived with my sister and my father and they were my whole world. I did not think of Cathy as a girl nor as a woman, I thought of her as Cathy. I did not think of Daddy as a man, though I knew that he was. I thought about him, likewise, as Daddy.

In the months I lived with Daddy and Cathy in the copse I let my hair grow long. It was long through inattention. I did not think to cut it. I did not think to ask Cathy or Daddy to cut it for me. They did not prompt me. So it grew long. The colour of beech bark. And matted, for want of a comb. And in places the hair was lank with oil for, though I washed it,

I could not wash it regularly. My nails were long too. I do not remember ever using nail scissors. I do not know if we had them in the house. When they became too much I picked and bit at them, trimming them roughly in that way. But with the exception of this occasional, inattentive grooming, I allowed the nails to grow. Not absurdly long, but slightly longer than, I discovered later, was appropriate for a boy. Or for a man. I did not know then that it was girls not boys who grew their hair and their nails long. I did not think about it. Nor did I realise that the men and boys who lived nearby would never wear a T-shirt that did not reach their jeans, as I did. Partly, again, this was through inattention. I had grown taller without noticing but still wore the same T-shirts. But partly, I have to admit, I wore my clothes in this manner because I had seen my mother wearing her clothes in this manner. I wore those little T-shirts and those too-tight jeans and I left my midriff bare because I had seen my mother do this. And nobody corrected me. Or nobody noticed. Or it did not matter. Or I do not know what.

So when I picked up some of Vivien's underwear that time and I went upstairs to use the bathroom, and I held it up and looked at the lace and examined the pale residue at the gusset, it was not like it would have been were I a grown man walking into a woman's bedroom uninvited and doing those things.

I assure you, it was not the same. I was not a threat. How could I have been?

I did not know about etiquette, nor about the correct and proper ways in which men and women should conduct themselves. Nor did I have any understanding that there were parts of the body that held a different worth, a different kind of value or category. And that those body parts were guarded with different kinds of clothing, and that some of the value or meaning of those body parts rubbed off on their prescribed clothes.

In short, I did not know what it was that I was doing.

And besides, my interest was not the same interest as the interests of real men.

So my actions cannot be categorised in the same way.

I heard Vivien upstairs again. She left her bedroom and went to the bathroom. She had put on the light. I could hear the breezy, oscillating hum of the extractor fan.

I got up out of my armchair and went over to the fireplace. I took the iron poker from its stand. Its handle had been too close to the flames and was hot to touch. I could only just hold it. I stabbed it into the heart of the glowing, fizzing coals. I held it there.

I held it there for too long. The temperature of the iron was drawn from almost bearable to just unbearable and my grip instinctively loosed. The poker fell to the hearth and rang with a hollow harmony.

Vivien heard. 'Is everything all right down there?' she called.

I did not respond. Presumably, despite my silence, she was not concerned enough to repeat her enquiry nor to come down.

I thought about what I would need to do to get her to come rushing down. I covered my hand, still somewhat tender, with the sleeve of my pullover and reached down to grab the poker once again. I hesitated. It would be too much to use the poker to knock the coals onto the carpet. I was banking on the rug catching fire, or at least some strong charring, but knocking coals off the grate might do more damage than I could predict or control. All of Vivien's furniture, paintings, books, could be incinerated. Then she would be forced to run down the stairs in her dressing gown or whatever.

I put the poker back in its stand and went into the kitchen. Vivien kept her best china plates on display on the upper shelves of an oak Welsh dresser. She had told me the maker once, and the age of the plates, and she had told me that they had been a wedding present to her great grandparents from a distant aunt.

They could all be ripped from their positions with one sweep of my arm. They would shatter on the counter surface of the lower cabinet, else cascade to the slate tiles and shatter there. The delicate, hand-limned indigo flowers and maroon leaves in disarticulated pieces on the floor. Vivien would hear the commotion from upstairs and come rushing down.

It would be thrilling, to be sure. But ultimately I knew that I would not be able to stand the censure. She would run down the stairs and see me standing among the shards of her family heirloom. My heart-beat would quicken, I am certain that it would. There would be a terrific excitement in it. But then the excitement would curdle. I would see her incredulity, her despair, her ire, and my guilt would first creep then rush to meet my elation, deep in the pit of my guts.

I took the kettle off its stand, filled it with water then placed it back and flicked the switch. At first the filament simply hummed but soon the water stirred. The gurgle of the water and the roar of the shooting steam were enough to mask the sound of my footsteps. I gently climbed the staircase.

Vivien's bedroom was next to the bathroom and the door was half open. She stood in a bra and slip. The bra was black with lace trim. The slip was cream and silky. The thick tan waistband of her flesh-coloured tights was visible above the slip and it pinched her tummy. The place just below the thinnest part of her waist, where she would have kept her baby had she been pregnant, bulged against the cream satin. She had combed her hair and there was a slight, deliberate kink in it. The kink caught the incandescent light in her bedroom and turned it radiant gold.

She stood by the mirror and leaned as she applied mascara to her eyelashes.

She had not seen me. She had not heard me. The kettle sang. I backed away, back across the landing and down the stairs.

Half an hour or so later she came down in full dress. She was beautiful.

IV

*I talk to Bill more than I should. I ramble. I distract
him from the road. I talk to him about Cathy and
about Daddy, about our house on the hill, about
the woods and trees, about the food we ate and the
cider we drank. I talk to him about the friends we
made and the animals we kept. I tell him everything.
Everything that happened that night.*

*I was tired of walking, and Bill was also travelling
north. Meet her at the destination, he said to me.
Find her at the end of the line.*

*I jumped up into his cab and we drove into the
night.*

*I am his radio. I stutter and burble and fizz with
the telling. And then I fall silent as I lose myself in
thought.*

It is rightly a two hour ride to Edinburgh, but this stranger weaves a crooked path. He takes back roads and diagonals and hops from town to town and village to village to deliver his cargo. I see more of the country than I had known was there. All the better to search for her, he said. You don't know where she's gone, he said. In that he might be right.

We pass over hills of heather in purple. We see the great rock illuminated from miles away and the ebb and surge of the grizzled North Sea.

Eyes blue like the North Sea, Daddy once said of my sister. Eyes blue like the North Sea.

Bill talks to me about the marks on his body. He once caught the wrong end of a lit soldering iron when he was still at school and the palm of his hand has melted like wax and stretched over the flexing bones. Part of his toe is missing on his left foot, lost to a mis-struck hammer. A jagged scar runs the length of his right thigh from when he fell while scaling a barbed fence. There are marks on his face from fights. Nothing proper, mind. Not like Daddy's fights. Just scraps. There are peppered dots on his eyeballs from an infection when he was young. Otherwise the irises are the brown and grey of West Yorkshire sandstone, flecked likewise with the soot of industry.

I spot myself in the grimy rain-flecked wing-mirrors of Bill's cab, leaning against the passenger's window smeared with the grease from my cheeks *and fingerprints and the grease and fingerprints of whoever has come before me. I am hollow. Distorted. Out of focus. Out of frame. The world rushes behind my image. Beside me Bill tells more tales. Issues with contractors. News from the world of haulage. People jumping out of the container when he opens up the back after a sea crossing. People even he did not know were there.*

We stop on a back road somewhere in the Borders. We will continue in the morning. We settle for the night. He tells me that when he first saw me he thought I was a wee girl. A wee girl alone by the side of the road.

I turn out to face the window. There is mist on the pane. The street beyond is dark and damp and limned with a humble glow.

This man who is older than my Daddy takes my hand in his.

I hold my breath.

Chapter Fifteen

Mr Royce said the bonfire had galvanised the community. Cathy and I took this as a good thing. Now, he said, it was a case of turning that good will into action.

Mr Royce set about organising the farm labourers. They would demand better pay. The landowners round here had been holding them in check with the threat of shopping them for benefits fraud, but Mr Royce said if enough of them stuck together, with good evidence that the bosses were complicit in their activities, their threats would come to nothing. The landowners would try to hire work from elsewhere to fill the gaps. The potatoes needed sorting, the fruit needed picking, the summer months were here and harvest was approaching. The fields could not be left unworked.

They met in the mornings at the usual pick-up spots but instead of climbing into the vans, they handed their foreman a sheet of paper on which they had written their demands. Mr Royce had helped them with this. He had experience from the miners' strikes, though this was a smaller group, and I heard Mr Royce admit quietly to Daddy one evening that it might be too small a group to make a difference and that the work they did was too easily replaced.

It was hoped that the withholding of rents would make more of a difference. More families could participate in this. People who lived in houses that the council had built and once owned but which Mr Price or his friends had since bought up. The rents were higher than most could afford and everyone in the neighbouring villages – old pit villages – had accrued debts with Price and the others. Debts that they feared could be called in at any time, in any number of ways.

Daddy went with Mr Royce to each house in turn. Many had been there with us for the bonfire and those that had not had heard of the plans through other avenues. Daddy and Mr Royce told each one that everyone was going to stop paying their rents, and instead the money they would usually give over to Mr Price or the other landlords would be collected into a central fund. This was to help people in times of need and Mr Royce said in private that it would be good for just in case. Just in case things did not go their way and in the end everyone had to pay up anyway. Again, he did not admit this to the group, just in discussion with Martha and Daddy, to which Cathy and I always listened in.

Daddy got drunk on cider one evening on the fat grass outside our house. He said to us or to himself or to the house or to the trees or to the birds in the branches that we were all fools. He said it was all just vanity, that it was Ewart's vanity for thinking this sort of thing could still make a difference and that it was his vanity for thinking he could protect them all, while still keeping us safe, along with our house on the hill. These were old dreams, he said, and should have been left as just that.

The next morning, however, he got up early and made his usual rounds of the villages, to reassure people, to see if there had been any mischief, to make sure that these people knew this man was still on their side. He was gone for more than three hours but when he returned his mood was optimistic. 'We might just be able to break bastards,' he told us.

Mr Royce's mood varied as well. Sometimes when he came up to visit us or we went down to him in the village he wore a glum demeanour, a deeply stifled terror. But usually he was hopeful about the operation and spoke at length about the positive responses he had had, and about how all the signs were, for the moment, positive.

News came that Gerald Castor had already raised the men's wages. Mr Royce had gone along with the labourers to the pick-up point in the morning and argued the case with the foreman himself. Gerald Castor had come down from the farm to speak with them. 'My arguments got better of him, dindt they?' Mr Royce said. 'He were unprepared and he got spooked when I started talking about law. That's thing. You just have to seem official, seem like you know what you're talking about – well I, as a matter of fact, I do know what I'm talking about, but unfortunately seeming like you do is often just as important – and, yes, then they don't know what to do with themselves. That's how it were. Castor were taken off-guard and said that if men come next day they'll be paid what we agreed – what all landowners should be paying their workforce. These farmers and landlords have clubbed together, led by Price, but without him and each other they're nothing. That's what we must remember.'

We congratulated Mr Royce and had some of the men round to ours for a drink. It was a kind of celebration but it was also to make sure they connected this victory in their minds with our house, and the words that had been spoken here at the bonfire weeks before. It would be no use if they went back to work but forgot to remember the other people they were fighting with and the other people they were fighting against. Mr Price was the real enemy, Daddy always said, but perhaps that only really applied to us.

He did tell Cathy and me one evening that though he cared deeply about everyone else involved in this, he could not help but fixate exclusively on my and Cathy's house. That's how he sometimes referred to it, as Cathy's and mine, like he did not truly inhabit it. It was like he forgot to say that it was ours, as a family, or like he forgot he could live in a home, like he forgot about his need to settle and live comfortably and be looked after by my sister and me.

He told us that was why he was really in on all of this. To protect us, to get our house for us, and to keep our lives within it safe forever. He said that this was very bad, and that we were not to let anyone know, but if it came down to it he would do anything to see us right. 'The others be damned,' he said once, very quietly.

The good news continued. A few days after the incident with Gerald Castor, Mr Royce came up to see us with news that another farmer had accepted their demands, Jeremy Higgins. And then a couple of days after that, there was another.

For that first couple of weeks it seemed too easy. The men were all asking each other why they had not done anything like this before. They had assumed their work was worth nothing. Many were just out of prison or else serially unemployed. They thought rough labour out on a farm for cursory, under-the-table payment was all they could get. And possibly they were right. But still the landlords needed them. It was not like they were doing these men a favour. Yet, what with the new wages, the employers could have gone and got other people to work for them, but they did not want the paperwork. Our lot still were not asking for contracts or anything like that, you see. It had been discussed by everyone, including Mr Royce, and everyone had decided against it. Nobody wanted to be on any kind of official radar, much. And that was not for tax reasons. It was just nobody wanted the authorities – least of all the police – to know anything about any of it. That held true for the farmers as much as for the workers. That was the pressure-point on which all of this seemed to operate. Both sides were trying to push each other but not so much as the police would get involved.

Given that, when the recriminations started, as Daddy warned they would, Mr Price's men did not hold back as there was no fear that we or any of the others would report it. After at first agreeing to the demands, both Gerald Castor and Jeremy Higgins and any of the others who had initially conceded, then went back on their words. It was suspected, with good reason, that they had consulted with each other and then with Price, and – though cowed by the initial shock of the workers' and Mr Royce's activities – had then thought again, taken stock, composed some kind of plan.

Reports came that they were hiring work from elsewhere. Bussing people in. Standard practice, said Mr Royce, you just had to know how to handle it. We had to find out where they were getting them from and where they were being picked up and dropped off. I did not learn what the plan was after that.

The real fuss arrived when the end of the month came and went and no rents had been paid from any of the houses in the entire area. That was a bigger deal. Mr Royce said it would be. That was where the real money lay, he said, and up here it was a lot harder to get new tenants than new workers.

There were recriminations. Mr Price and some of the others employed men all year round to collect their rents and sort out their problems. They were big men, strong and mean. If a tenant got behind with his or her payments they would come round and see to it. They were full-time, private bailiffs. They would knock on the door. They would make threats. If still the money did not come they would knock down the door and take what was owed in kind. They were hard men, big and tough and ruthless. But they were nothing to Daddy.

Daddy was king. A foot taller than the tallest of

these men, Daddy was gargantuan. Each of his arms was as thick as two of theirs. His fists were near the size of their heads. Each of them could have sat curled up inside his ribcage like a foetus in a mother's womb. These men did not move Daddy, and when they began prowling in earnest, he knew how to respond.

The bailiffs started knocking on doors. At first they would concentrate on a few houses in a certain area. This made it easy for Daddy. Gary, our man from the potato sorting, had use of his uncle's car and as soon as he got a call from any of the tenants he would drive Daddy over as quickly as he could. Daddy would get out and make his hulking presence known. The bailiffs would leg it.

So the bailiffs started mixing up their routine. They would only go to one house in a neighbourhood and then get in their cars and drive away before Gary and Daddy could get there. But Daddy stepped it up as well. When he did catch up with a couple of them he dragged them down a snicket into a patch of overgrown grass, laced with wild flowers, cut off from view by high hawthorns. There, he broke ribs and fingers and sent them on their way.

Daddy did that a couple of times with a couple of different groups of them. The bailiffs began to lose interest. For them it was just a job, after all. They were only getting paid. And the landlords couldn't pay them enough to make risking their necks worthwhile, not without paying out to bailiffs more than they would make back in rents.

It seemed as if we were winning. Morale was high. We met regularly, up at our house, to drink and chat and urge each other on. There was a real spirit behind it all, and people were excited.

But, of course, it could not last. And on a Tuesday, late on in the evening, but not so as it was yet dark, Mr Price drove up to our house.

I was scuffing up the path when Mr Price drove his Land Rover up the hill. There had been heavy summer rains this last fortnight and the torrents had run down the slope with half a tonne of mud, silt and rocks, and had pooled at the bottom of our path near where it met the bridleway. I had taken a rusted iron rake from the tool-shed and was shunting sediment back into a path shape. It was all clay up here. The claggy earth clung to the teeth of my rake as I scraped it into place, such that I could barely see the metal through the topsoil.

I heard Mr Price's jeep coming up the bridleway. I knew of no one else with an engine that grand and smooth. He turned the corner onto our path and the front wheels of his vehicle sunk right far into the standing sludge. That deep engine revved and the wheels spun for a bit, kicking up muck and water that would have splattered me had I not seen it coming. He did not dare take the hill, so slowly reversed back out onto the bridleway and parked the jeep on the verge.

He opened the door and stepped out. If he was flustered and bothered behind those blacked-out windows he did not show it when he stepped into the outside, out in the evening light. He came towards me with a sinking sun at his back, illuminated. 'You're just the man,' he said.

I stumbled. 'I think I'll just go and get my Daddy.'

'No, no, no.' He held out a hand to gather me back round, so as I would go with him out into the bridleway. His tone was sweet, generous. His face was kind.

I looked up at my house. The lights were being lit.

God, I was a coward sometimes.

Mr Price was still standing there, with his arm outstretched, waiting for me. It was a case of pleasing the person who was right there in front of me, you see.

I picked my way through the puddles and out into the lane. Mr Price took us to a place where we were hidden from the house by the honeysuckle.

He stood in front of me. He was wearing wellington boots, corduroy trousers, and in the warm summer evening just a chequered cotton shirt, unbuttoned at the top.

He put his left foot up on the banking and leaned

on it with his left elbow so that his whole posture opened and dipped. Like this, he stood a few inches smaller than me, and he looked up at me with brindle eyes.

I noticed that I was fidgeting with my hands and feet, rubbing the soles of my shoes back and forth against the damp grass and winding my fingers in rings about themselves.

'What's your surname, lad?'

'Oliver.'

'Daniel Oliver?'

'Yeah.'

'Daniel and Catherine Oliver.'

'Yeah. What of it?'

'What's your Daddy's surname?'

'Smythe.'

'Smythe?'

'Aye. You know that.'

Mr Price nodded. 'I do know that. I just wanted to ask.'

He shifted his weight so that he was standing tall, but there was still warmth in his manner as far as I could discern.

'You and your sister were given your mother's surname.'

'Aye. So what? That happens lots of times.'

'I suppose it does.' Mr Price paused and wetted his lips, looking at me the whole while. 'You see,

I've got a great deal more time for an Oliver than I do for a Smythe. It's fortunate for you, then, that that is what you are.'

I shrugged. 'I can't say I knew my mother all that well. Daddy's been both for us. Both mother and father. Daddy and our Granny Morley were, I mean. Before we came here. I might be an Oliver by name, but I'm a Smythe by nature.'

Mr Price considered these words for a moment and then shook his head, ever so slightly. 'No,' he said. 'No, I don't see that at all. You are not a bit like your father.'

An ounce of extra stubbornness shot through me with this declaration.

Mr Price continued: 'I don't suppose you're enjoying the current state of affairs much. I shouldn't think it would be in your nature to seek out or prolong proceedings such as these. The strike, I mean. This business about the rents for the properties I own. It's all a bit silly, isn't it? That's my take on it, if you want to know. It should never have come to this. Why are your father and his friends approaching things in this way, I ask myself? Why not just come to me straight away to discuss their grievances?'

'You threatened to kick us off our land, that's why.'

'Did I? You heard that, did you? You were there, were you?'

'No, I wandt there. But Daddy said.'

'Daddy said?'

'Aye.'

Mr Price gathered himself, folded his arms on his lower chest. 'I would give you this land tomorrow,' he said. 'This tiny copse with a handful of good trees and clay that's running down into the Levels? I would give it up to you tomorrow. Not to your Daddy, but to you. Not a Smythe, but an Oliver. Your Daddy is a brute. You are your mother's son. What do you say to that?'

'I . . . I don't really understand.'

'I'm telling you I would give you the land, where your Daddy's built that house, tomorrow. It would be yours, officially. I would sign over the papers. There would be no further problems.'

'But I woundt want it by myself. I would still want to live with Daddy and Cathy.'

'And I suppose that's it, right there. The thought of handing over your mother's land to your father doesn't sit well with me. Never has. But he just placed himself on it, didn't he? He'd been after it for years and then, one morning, he just turned up and started building. And the first I heard of it, he'd already got the best part of a house up. Does that sound right to you?'

I said nothing.

'You knew it was your mother's land, didn't you? Your father told you that much, surely?'

Still I was silent.

'You knew that she lived up here, all her life? She inherited the land from her parents. And when she fell on hard times – which you'll know all about, being her son – she came to me for help. And so I bought this land off her for a very high price indeed, and she should, would have been able to put herself back together again, start afresh, if it wasn't for your father. And although this land is rightfully mine, and even after all that your parents have put me through, both when your mother was alive, and now that it's just your father left causing me bother, I would happily sign it over to you, Daniel Oliver. I would give it to you out of the affection I held for the girl she was. But instead, your father seized it. He seized it from me when he had no right.'

I shrugged again. 'No one else was doing anything with land.'

'Maybe so. But that's not the way the world works. That's not how good, decent people operate.'

'We're decent people. We needed somewhere to live, is all.'

Mr Price looked me up and down and then walked around me towards his Land Rover. I thought he was going to drive away. I was feeling just a little bit proud of myself, like I had seen him off, like I had done one for the family, but he was not leaving just yet. He opened the door of the front passenger seat and reached into the glove compartment. He emerged with a clear plastic folder, containing a thick pad of documents, most in white, others in pastels: pink, yellow, blue, green.

'I have the documents here,' he said. 'I am willing to sign the land over, officially, to you, Daniel Oliver. Look, you're the named party.' He pointed to the wording on the opening page. I saw my name laid out in black block capitals. 'But knowing, as I do, that you would want to live here with your father – you are still a minor, after all – I have certain conditions. I need to know that your father isn't going to be as hostile a neighbour as he has shown himself to be in recent months. I don't want someone living so close to me who is going to give me a hard time, who is going to threaten my business and my property. Who would want that? Nobody. So you must tell him, first of all, that if he wants to be sure of a home for you all, and he wants the land to be in his son's name – because he can be sure it will never be in his name – he must call off this stupid business. He must get those scroungers back to work, and he must make sure those rents are paid. Now I've spoken to the local farmers, and we've all agreed to up the pay a little bit. That's only fair. And there won't be any increases in rent for the next two years, and then only in line with inflation. Do you know what that is? No, well never mind. I've laid it all out in here.' He waved the folder. 'Here's a letter to be given to your father, along with copies of the documents that I will sign if he agrees. That way he can think on it. He can weigh up the situation and make his decision. And then that'll be that. Done.'

I took the folder from him and tucked it under my arm. 'Are those conditions? That Daddy calls it all off?'

'Not entirely,' said Mr Price. 'Your Daddy must work for me, from time to time, as he always used to. He must return to the fold. I used to own that man's muscles, and I owned his mind. I owned his fists and his feet; his eyes and his ears and his teeth. How do you think he met your mother?'

'I've never really thought about it.'

Mr Price made no answer. He folded his arms then unfolded them, and then placed them on his hips. 'Just you get that message to your father,' he said, pointing at my chest. 'Tell him that's all I want from him. I want to use him again. Him and that great, hulking body, the like of which I've never seen, not in this county, not in this country. Tell him I want to see those muscles tested, and those fists put to their proper use. Aye, I know he'll never go round the houses for me, knocking about whoever I want him to knock about, like he might have done when he was a pup. But tell him I've got prouder work for him, if he'll do it. Tell him I've found a man for him to fight.'

He turned his back on me and went back to his jeep. He drove away. Mud spat like shrapnel.

I had left my rake sticking straight up from the silt. It was the wrong tool for the job. I suckered it out of the ground, swung it over my right shoulder and bobbed up the hill to our house.

The front door was swinging, caught on a small, bouncing breeze with no particular direction. Cathy had left the door hanging so that this light, dewy wind could sweep the floors for us, and dance through the curtains, and the nooks in the walls, and leave our home with soft freshness and the smell of damp pollen and snapped greenwood.

'Done with dredging?' asked Daddy.

'Nope. I was interrupted.'

I passed him the folder. He looked down at it and then up at me.

'It's from Price. He was here. He told me to tell you he wants to come to some kind of accord. He wants you to work for him, only not like you think. He said he's got someone for you to fight. And then he'll give us the land – he'll sign it over to us. He said he'd do that.'

'He said that? That he'd provide documents for the land.'

'Yes. For us.'

'For us all?'

'For me. He said he'd sign the land over to me. I

dindt fully understand. But it amounts to same thing. It'll be ours on paper, and that means something.'

Daddy looked again at the folder, and took the documents from within. He looked at them closely, placing the pages flat on the table and leaning over them. He traced his index finger on the words, one by one, mouthing them precisely as he read. After some minutes he pushed the paper aside.

'Means nothing to me.'

'I can help,' I said tentatively.

He shook his head. 'No, lad, it's not that. I can read well enough to understand what it says. It's idea a person can write summat on a bit of paper about a piece of land that lives and breathes, and changes and quakes and floods and dries, and that that person can use it as he will, or not at all, and that he can keep others off it, all because of a piece of paper. That's part which means nowt to me.'

Daddy gathered the documents and shuffled them back into the folder. The heels of the chair-legs scraped as he stood. The large man slouched as he went to the front door.

'I'll think on it,' he said as he left the house and made for the copse.

Chapter Sixteen

The note came early before we were up. Cathy found it in the hall. It had been slipped under the door. She made breakfast and placed the note on the kitchen table, a hatchet that cut its way between the glass milk jug and the enamel coffee pot.

I woke with the smell of bacon in my nose. Daddy emerged from his bedroom too and followed the scent. He saw the note as I came through the open door into the kitchen. He pinched it between thumb and forefinger and lifted it. He saw that it was addressed to him, sliced the envelope with the bread-knife and opened it.

'Mr Price?' Cathy asked. The coffee had stewed for too long and a dark brown, opaque liquid oozed from the spout.

Daddy hocked his throat for the first time that morning and spat up the residue glued to his windpipe by the night's humidity and a slow evening cigarette.

'He's called me out.'

'A fight?'

'Yes, more or less. He's arranged it as if it's nothing more than a matter of business. There'll be prize money and men will be allowed to bet on it. But, of course, we know that it handt got owt to do with business this time. He wants me to fight for him. If I win, he'll get a lot of money and he'll sign this land over to you two. If I lose, well, I'm sure he'll still get a lot of money. He manages to fix things that way.'

It was to be held in the woods overlooking the racecourse. There was some precedent in that. For hundreds of years travellers had toured the racecourses, buying and selling horses, tackle, and entertainments when the racing was over and the nights fell. Then the course would be given over to travellers and their friends. Lights would be lit, meat roasted, and whisky drunk. And fights fought.

These days, the woods behind the racecourse offered cover from the police and from passers-by. Dog-walkers rarely entered the woods, such was the reputation.

*

Daddy trained in the copse to find his form. He lifted what he could find – logs, stones – until some people clubbed together to bring up some second hand dumbbells. He lifted me up too, as if I weighed nothing at all, as if there had been no change in my weight since the day I was born and he had lifted me out of my mother's arms.

He ate more meat and fish, almost double what he had been eating before. And he walked and ran to improve his endurance. That was more important now, more than ever, he said. He knew how hard he could hit and how quickly his punches could find their mark but if his opponent was much younger he would run around him and tire him out then if Daddy made a mistake, he might fall.

He told me one evening of his fears. He made sure that Cathy was out, as she often was, and he spoke to me unusually clearly. He said that he was worried he was too old. He said that there was no greater burden than success, that he had an unbeaten record and a reputation that extended well beyond the boundaries of England and Ireland. In the right circles, at any rate. But fighting while weighed down with that record, he said, would be more difficult than ever. And he worried, because this fight really meant something.

In previous bouts that he fought for money he could go in without any expectation. Even though others might stake their savings on him to win, he did not have to care unless he wanted to. He could remain calm, almost casual, and he would win because he could afford to be reckless.

Now there was more at stake. Much more than just money. And he was older. 'Old muscle,' he said, as he patted his biceps.

I told him that if he lost it would not matter to me and that we would find another way to keep the house, and remove the Prices from our lives. And if we could not, then we could always move away, start again, and we would still be together.

I walked down to Vivien's house with the pups the evening before the fight. The mood in my house was tight; Daddy had gone to the copse and Cathy just sat on the step smoking. I wanted out. Blackbirds sung in the hedgerows as dusk settled. The dogs felt the twilight too. They were uneasy with the coming darkness.

The light was bright in Vivien's hall and as I crossed the threshold I caught the aroma of the evening primrose that surrounded the entrance.

'I thought I'd see you this evening,' she said. She hurried as she spoke, and looked over my shoulder as she ushered me inside. The dogs kept to my heel, unsure of the new scents.

The house was colder than it had been outside. An upstairs window clattered in its frame. The sound of wood on wood, like a glockenspiel, bounced down the stairs. The net curtains rustled. Vivien hurried about, shutting everything up, pinning the latches, tucking in the material, closing velvet outer curtains, bolting shutters where there were shutters. She took Jess and Becky from me and bustled them into the kitchen, took off their leads and stored them in a drawer, took out bowls from the cupboard and filled them with water and the remains of her own beef stew from the casserole on the hob. She closed the door behind them. They did not try to follow her out but began to lap up water, tails wagging in easy delight.

She moved towards me, gripped my elbow and pushed me into a chair. Serious, I thought, but when she spoke her voice held its regular sweet lilt.

'I thought I'd see you this evening,' she said again. 'You're going off to the fight tomorrow, aren't you? Your father is set on it, then?'

'I believe so. Why do you ask?'

'Because I think it's a risk,' she said, bluntly. 'I've seen the man he is facing and I think your father could lose.'

I did not know what to say. Certainty had been running away from me for weeks.

'Why will he lose?'

'Because he'll be fighting against a much younger man.'

'A man who's inexperienced, then. A man who's not been tested.'

'Oh, he's certainly been tested, but not around here so your Daddy wouldn't know him. He's been brought over from Eastern Europe. Ukraine. I think you should urge him to pull out,' she continued. 'I'm worried about him. He won't feel the shame of it, I know. For a man like him, who lives the life he leads, he's remarkably unconcerned by shame.'

'But he has to. He has to for others. And for house.'

She was paler than she had been when we had first met. Clots of black mascara had smudged onto her eyelids.

'So you won't?'

I shook my head, and soon after got up to leave. She did not attempt to change my mind. She knew what we were all like, Daddy, Cathy and me. She hugged me on the way out, for a long time. I half thought she was going to kiss me on the cheek but she did not. She put her hand briefly through my hair and gave me a gentle nudge out the door.

I ran back along the road with the dogs and up the hill as the evening settled in earnest. I saw swifts darting around catching the small flies that had just slipped from their chrysalises. Jess and Becky had grown tall and lean these last months, with all their power stored in their taut back legs. They chased around me and each other in huge loping circles as I stuck to the path.

I returned to find that Daddy had gone to bed early. Cathy was still up in the kitchen, smoking. She was excited and awake and alive. The thought of Daddy losing had not flown through her. She was as bright as ever I had seen her.

That night, I lay awake staring at the wall in the dim moonlight, at the creases and crevices left by my father's rough plasterwork, at his thumb prints, finger prints, the curve of his pallet knife, the sweep of the plaster that matched the motion of his right arm.

When I did sleep I dreamt of a long walk home beneath the calls of roosting starlings.

Chapter Seventeen

The dawn erupted from a bud of mauve half-light and bloomed bloody as I woke. My lips stretched to a wide yawn as I sucked into my warming lungs the cool breeze that threaded a path through the open window. My eyes were tired and I saw the room in rapid stills through flickering lashes. Condensed sweat adhered the frayed cotton bed sheets to my bare skin. I had glowed hot during the night, hot from fitful dreams and restless limbs, and now shivered in the comparative chill.

I rose and wove cautious steps into the wet room. We had no shower but a stiff tap to release hot water. It gushed intermittently. The power came from a wood-burning boiler, lit each morning by whoever woke first. It heated sufficient water for three to pigeon wash, spilling the water into a bucket beneath the tap and onto the stone floor as we cast it under our armpits, our groins, our necks, faces and ears, our feet, and our legs, arms and torsos.

I splashed the steaming water onto my sticky skin and stroked it lightly with a bar of soap. My hands puckered red and white but I held them still beneath the tap. I rinsed my body and dried it with a small square of towel then slipped myself into fresh and crinkled clothes.

I stepped out into the hall and caught the sour scent of kippers poaching in milk. We ate them with white, buttered bread and fresh orange juice, a gift from the milkman.

At 7 o'clock, we heard the sound of Ewart Royce's Volvo estate on the coarse gravel outside. The wheels slowed and stopped before we heard the brakes. Two doors shunted open then clipped shut. A knock echoed from the door. Cathy opened it.

'Your car.' Ewart looked darker, older, more stern. Nerves treated people differently. Our anxieties were focussed on the same target but each from a different angle and with their own tints.

Martha waited by the vehicle and opened the boot as we stepped out with the bags and the dogs. Daddy climbed into the front seat and Martha got in behind him. Ewart was to drive, Cathy took the right-hand back seat and I sat in the middle between my sister and Mrs Royce.

We were bashed together as the car took the choppy track down our hill. The journey was hardly smoother on the open roads. In these parts they were puckered with potholes from icy winters and acid rain. On the worst roads the potholes were connected by cracks that had filled with sediment and organic material, compacted by passing cars before the weeds had managed to fully breach the tarmac. It made for a rough ride.

We spoke very little. Martha issued a handful of directions to Ewart and Ewart spoke once to ask for the time. Otherwise we were quiet. Cathy gazed out the window with her nose pressed gently against the smeared glass. Daddy breathed deeply. He did not turn his head. The back of his neck was covered with a film of perspiration that sparkled so clearly it was as if it had frozen into minuscule crystals of ice.

I glanced around at my companions, more interested in them than I ever could be by the world outside. After ten minutes of driving Martha reached over and gripped my left hand. Her palm was hot. I felt the steady pulse in her thumb and a warm band of gold on her ring finger. Her firm fingernails were set in acrylic.

We arrived at the racecourse forty-five minutes after leaving our house. We took the track around the perimeter fence to the grove behind. We drove between the trees, ash and oak like in our own copse.

Brittle, fallen twigs and branches snapped beneath our wheels. The track was too narrow. Brackens, ferns and wild garlic had overtaken its sides and pressed against the vehicle's body.

We came to a fork in the road. One route had been churned by previous cars, vans and four-by-fours. The other was strangely smooth, almost untouched. It was as if it had been flooded and the waters had soaked into the ground and evaporated into the air, leaving an even layer of sticky silt on that track and that track only, like a heavy toffee glaze.

As the car turned into the right fork I craned my neck to look back to the unused path. It was barren, more a strip of diseased or salted earth than a walkway. It led into a clearing where grass could find sunshine and push through the compressed earth and netted moss.

It slipped from view, obscured by the low-hanging branches of a particularly squat oak. I turned back in my seat and saw the cold sweat on Daddy's neck.

We rounded a corner into another clearing, this one muddy from rain and footfall. Vehicles were parked in a semi-circle around the edge, most with their boots open to the slight drizzle. Men, a few boys and girls, and a very few women, stood around the open boots, peering. The fair was a chance to buy and sell. For many that might have been the main event. There were pedigree puppies and assorted rare breeds of ornamental chickens. There was a large Land Rover in one corner that was flanked by men with shaved heads and bomber jackets and most people stayed well clear. Guns possibly. Or bombs or pornography.

'Cathy, Danny, you two get out first,' said Daddy. 'Find somewhere quiet to stand.'

I slid out behind Cathy and sank my boots into the mud. We trudged the outer rim. People stood around and swayed like the hulking trees that enveloped the gathering. They chatted and smoked and exhibited their animals, tools, weapons. Someone had set up a fire in an oil drum with a griddle to cook sausages and onions. Cathy and I shifted in the direction of the savoury smoke and spitting fat only to be turned away when we confessed we had no money.

'What do you think this is? A food bank? Get out of it!'

Instead we loitered around the back of a black transit van that was filled with barrels of live fish. Goldfish, catfish, carp, perch. All swimming in water. The barrels were labelled, along with the approximate ages of the fish and the prices. Angling was big business around here.

Fighting, fishing and animals. That is where these people put their money.

I took a chance and stepped up into the van to take a closer look at what was on offer. There they were, at the bottom of the barrel. Fish the length of my forearm, spiralling up and down and around one another. Making the best use of the space they had. A pipe pumped air into the bottom of the barrel and it burbled up and tickled their gills and loose scales as the fish passed through the stream, gulping for sustenance.

'Here, get out of it,' said a sharp voice from behind me. It was a skinny little ginger boy a head shorter than Cathy. His face was shaded by sandy freckles and acne scabs. He wore an indigo tracksuit and white trainers. There was a residue of masticated toast stuck between his front teeth. 'You can't go in there unless you're serious about buying. And you two aren't buying owt.'

'Who's going a buy live fish here anyway?' said Cathy. 'Who'd come see a fight an buy a couple of carp?'

'Who asked you, you stupid bitch?'

Any other day Cathy might have smacked him one. She spat through her teeth and her cheeks had filled with colour.

Her cheeks reddened readily, like mine. We both resented it. How I wished I could stay an icy pale when angry or excited.

She stepped back and walked away quickly.

I hurried after her, ignoring the sound of a heavy ball of mucus and saliva hitting the ground behind my feet as I turned.

She was pacing quickly, right across to the other side of the clearing where the serious business was happening, where Mr Price was talking with Daddy. Talking terms, outcomes, rules of sorts. Where the other serious men were standing around, their hands in the pockets of their waxed jackets, or round the leads of vicious-looking dogs. 'Dogs in the cars when the fight's on,' I heard someone say. I thought of Jess and Becky doing battle with a couple of these dogs, in defence of their respective masters. I thought about the power of a true dog bite, or the slash of a claw, so much worse than the playful nips a dog could give when jumping at your hand. I thought about blood and flesh mixed with a dog's saliva, and the tartar from its unbrushed teeth like blood mixed with rusted, dirty metal out on a farm far from help.

Daddy was unbuttoning his jacket, getting ready. I saw his opponent for the first time and felt acid in my throat.

He could have been six foot ten. He could have been taller. And he was heavy. He was sitting on the back of Mr Price's trailer with his feet planted firmly in the mud. His weight pitched the trailer, testing its suspension to the full such that its chassis almost touched the dirt.

There he was, slouched like a dancing bear propped against a wall, rubbing his knuckles, bulbous and calcified like Daddy's.

He caught sight of me staring as I pursued Cathy and pulled his lips up to his gums to reveal a full set of gold teeth. I looked quickly ahead. Cathy was heading for the trees.

I called after her like we were back at school. 'Wait up. Wait up!'

Another couple of steps and I could reach her shoulder. 'Wait up,' I said. 'Where you going? Fight's about to start.'

Cathy turned and looked over my shoulder to where the serious men were puffing and panting and moving around each other in ever decreasing circles. The crowd was beginning to swell. A slack loop was forming and the gaps were filling with men, like doves flying into the niches of their cote. Their shoulders locking. The abstract sound of the chatter had been administrative but was now hoarse with a kind of giddy terror.

'I don't want to watch it. I'm fed up. I'm fed up with the whole ruddy show.'

With that she stalked off into the trees. I saw her weaving a path between them until the cover of their trunks and branches tightened, slicing segments out of her torso until the screen became complete and she was out of sight.

I felt the men churning behind me. I did not want to return though knew simply that I should. There was a call to witness.

I turned my back on the woods and joined the other men. The lot of us trembled together.

The Bear was pacing and jumping to keep warm and stretching his muscles and shaking his bones. Daddy stood still. As still as a wolf. His eyes were glossier and bluer in the cold air and crisp grey light. They were fixed on his prey.

A referee came between the fighters and spoke intently to each man in turn then stepped back.

The Bear began to skip back and forth. His fists were raised. Daddy remained still, almost weary, despondent. He glanced over at me for the first time since we had arrived then raised his fists too. He made circles with them like an old Victorian pugilist whose motions were captured in stills. This is how he had learnt to fight, I remembered. He had told us once. He had learnt to fight at the hands of a very very old man who could barely stand but directed his movements from an armchair by the hearth.

The Bear scuffed his feet on the ground. Daddy rocked back and forth. The muscles in his thighs were tense and poised.

A blow from the Bear, which Daddy ducked. He was lighter on his feet now, suddenly geared into action, off his heels.

They were circling. The Bear tried again. He lunged with his right fist then followed with his left. Daddy avoided the first and then parried, raising his own left fist to go at his opponent's chin. The Bear pulled back and Daddy missed. Some calls from the crowd then a sudden shiver of silence. Another miss from the Bear, then another. Daddy was saving his punches.

They skipped. A couple more goes at it then the Bear struck home. Not to Daddy's head but to his chest. The crowd winced and jeered in equal measure. It must have winded him. I felt winded too. He was shuddering backwards, off balance. The Bear came at him again with a right hook. Daddy ducked but was clipped on the left side of his skull. Another knock.

Daddy peeled back. He heaved the breath back into his lungs and straightened his spine. The Bear bared his teeth – a flash of gold – and Daddy went for them. A sharp jab. Blood. He took a second jab at the teeth, trying to tease at the same place. He had spotted a weakness. The Bear flashing a set of gold teeth meant he had had to replace his own set of teeth, which meant his gums had been permanently weakened, which meant that he could lose more. Again for the teeth but Daddy was blocked then both men pulled back panting.

A dog barked from the back seat of a car and others joined the chorus.

The Bear caught Daddy hard on his left cheekbone with a blow that came from nowhere. A quiet crack

219

like a splitting log and then there was blood around his eye and dripping down his cheek, pooling on his shoulder and chest, on his white cotton vest. Daddy was blowing clots of blood from his nostrils like a dragon breathing fire.

He could not use that eye any more. It was swelling and closing up his eyelid.

But he kept on.

The slap of shoes against the mud. Men stamping and rubbing their hands. Daddy and the Bear, their fists in guard. Barking dogs. Spitting men. A sticky wind. Ancient oaks arching their backs to cover the scene. The scent of diesel. Diesel, dirt, sweat, blood, burning meat, the sugars dripping from fried onions. A ring of men standing above rings of mushrooms, connected and hidden beneath the earth, and then rings of limestone.

The Bear had Daddy on the back foot, dragging his heels. I tried hard not to look but I could not help it. Daddy's arms were dropping and his legs slipping. He was tired. He was tired and stooping.

Daddy gulped as if his breath was caught in his throat. The Bear came in for another punch. Daddy looked as though he barely had enough left in him to avoid the fist, but he did, for the most part. He was caught on his left shoulder, knuckle hit muscle.

But the Bear had overbalanced, and Daddy hooked round with his right fist. He moved his whole body behind the punch. He swung into it from his hips. He rose up on his haunches, almost up off his toes and off the ground. He was suddenly fresh again. A feint – perhaps it had been – a feint. His good eye was alert. He planted his fist on the other man's jaw with every estimation of strength he had.

Again a sound like splitting wood but this time not one cut cleanly with an axe but ripped from the side of a tree by lightning and thunder and wind. Wood that was shattering into a hundred pieces. A torrent of red and gold. Blood bursting from the Bear's unstoppered gums as his gold incisors, his gold canines, gold molars followed a long, slow arc to the sodden earth.

The Bear stumbled. I stumbled. I felt like I was going to pass out. Either pass out or piss myself. Oh no, oh please God no. There could be nowt worse. I rearranged my feet to steady myself and looked away, up at the sky, hoping that the cold breeze would catch my eyeballs and freshen me. Bring tears perhaps. Tears were better, tears from the cold, it could be. Oh god, please don't let me faint. Please. My insides were moving too now. My bowels. Oh please, God, no.

The huge man was falling, following his teeth into the mud. His eyes had rolled back into his skull. He was knocked out. And as he fell I felt dizzier and dizzier, like I'd been sucked inside him and was feeling the same motion, like I was falling too.

The Bear was on the ground. His head had slapped and cracked again. The men around me were moving forwards and so was the ground. I was about to fall.

And then I was in Daddy's arms. I had not seen him come for me. He had knocked out the Bear, he had won the fight, and almost in the same step come to me. He picked me up clean off the ground like I was his trophy. He raised me into the cold air. I felt the tears on my cheeks but no giddiness. I breathed deeply. No more sickness.

Our men were all around. And Peter, and Ewart and then Martha came over, carrying a zipped green bag, and she was opening it and taking out bandages and iodine and frozen peas.

From my vantage point in Daddy's arms I looked down to see his adversary lying on the floor, men crowding round him, doing little to help. One had a bucket of water and some cloths.

And then I saw Price. He was looking up at me. Staring at me as calmly as he had watched the whole fight. Just staring.

But where was Cathy? Where was Cathy?

As Daddy brought me back down, I looked to the perimeter of the woods. Had she come back after all? Had she watched the fight from the cover of the trees? Had she heard it?

Martha was fussing. She was pulling Daddy over to the car. She had fully opened up the boot of the

Volvo estate and laid out some towels. Jess and Becky came to greet us, yapping at Daddy. His feet were not dragging now. He was stepping brightly. He sat down in the back of the car boot and Ewart picked up his feet and propped them on a crate. He began to untie Daddy's laces and pull his shoes off. His socks were wet and dirty and Ewart took those off as well and wrapped the exposed skin with a towel.

Martha had wrapped the frozen peas in a thin towel too and placed them over Daddy's eye for him to hold. She dabbed iodine onto small fluffy pieces of cotton wool and cleaned up the other cuts. Daddy winced as she did this. Small, specific pain inflicted with care can be worse than any other kind.

'Water,' said Daddy. I pulled out a flask from the cool-box. He drank a little then put down the flask. With his good eye he looked at Ewart, who reached inside his coat and pulled out a hip flask. Daddy took it and swigged. He swilled the first mouthful around in his mouth then spat it on the ground. He swallowed the second.

Martha took the ice pack away from his eye and inspected the cuts. 'It'll need stitches. I'll clean it before you put those peas back on.'

She did not use the iodine but a softer solution of salt and water.

I helped him take off his shirt and put one on clean. Then I wrapped a fleece round him and a blanket over that. He was sitting very still, sipping from the hip flask but mostly staring out into the trees beyond, smiling contentedly.

I thought about what Vivien had said that time. About how fighting made Daddy feel. About him needing it, body and mind both. He appeared satisfied now. If only she could see him. She had been wrong about the outcome. She had doubted him.

Cathy had not appeared but I was not too worried, then. I knew she would be safe, partly because she was tough and partly because she had walked into the woods, and her and I knew woods well. Ash and oak, like ours at home.

'Anyone spoken to Price yet?' asked Daddy.

'Not yet. We wanted to get you fixed up first. That's more important,' said Martha.

'Is he a man of his word?' asked Daddy.

Ewart considered. 'He's a man of his word when he's in public. He'll set everything right here in front of others, and then – by that alone – he'll be bound to it. And he's cause to be happy. He's won a huge amount of money here today. He's bested those Russians. You weren't the favourite today. For the first time ever, is that? Nah, Price should be thanking you.'

Daddy shook his head. 'I'm not so sure.' He looked up at me. 'What do you think, Daniel?'

I had no idea, but I was hopeful. 'I think you've

224

won your prize,' I said. 'I think we'll be going home and it really will be our home.'

He nodded, more trying to will my words into truth than out of agreement.

I got him a pair of boots and after putting them on he got up and walked over to a group of cars, one of which was pulling away carrying the Bear. Another man was picking the gold teeth out of the mud and putting them into a sealable plastic bag. Price was sitting in the driving seat of his Land Rover, speaking to a couple of men through the window. I could not read his expression.

He saw Daddy approaching and gestured for the other men to stand aside but remain close.

'Well there it is,' stated Price. The outcome, he meant. The conclusion.

Daddy nodded. 'There it is.'

Daddy waited for a moment for Price to continue. He had an offer to complete. But Price let Daddy wait. He wanted Daddy to have to ask. In a final attempt at humiliating and subjugating him, he wanted Daddy to ask.

'How about it then? How about the land? Can we tie it all up then? Make it official?'

'We can,' said Price. 'Gavin has the signed documents.' He nodded to one of the men he had been talking to. A dim-looking thug who pulled a black ring binder out of a briefcase he was carrying. From the ring binder he unclipped one of the plastic wallets and gave it to Daddy.

I could tell from the way he hesitated before taking it that he did not really understand the transaction. He did not know what the document meant but did not want to ask Price to explain it. He had no understanding of the way things worked in the real world and he had no experience with paper and the law.

Mr Price smirked. 'Those are the deeds, which I had signed, that formally give you the land that you have built that house on.'

'And the copse behind?' asked Martha sharply from behind. 'And with rights to access the road, I mean the track in front?'

Price considered for a moment. He would answer all our questions slowly, in his own time. 'Yes. You can read it if you like, though I hope you trust that I am a man of my word. It's all there.'

Martha took the plastic wallet out of Daddy's hands and pulled out the sheets of paper, which had been stapled at the corner. She began to read.

Mr Price tapped his steering wheel in irritation.

'We have to know what we're getting, Price,' said Martha without looking up at him. 'I'll have to read through all this, whether you like it or not, and you can't leave until I do.'

'Can't?'

She continued to read, flicking back and forth

through the papers when she came to a detail she needed to check.

Price did wait and after a minute or so commented idly to himself or perhaps to his men or possibly really to us, 'Strange, isn't it? An illegal fight to settle a legal dispute. Ending the day by signing papers after a spectacle that could have us all thrown in jail.'

Martha ignored him and continued to read, but Daddy looked up at him curiously, suspiciously. Ewart shuffled his feet, uneasily.

Martha finished reading. 'I think you should sign it. I will witness,' she said. They did so on the bonnet of Mr Price's Land Rover.

He drove away soon after with that smooth heavy purr of the Land Rover rolling slowly over wet ground. The sun was coming out and the dampness was lifting from the clearing in a thin haze that seemed to pulse evenly upwards from the crest of the trees. Slices of sunlight came through the clouds, the shape of a blackbird's singing beak.

Money was changing hands throughout the clearing. Every man there, it seemed, had placed a bet. The paper notes were shuffled, counted then folded hastily and placed into inside top pockets. The bookmakers' assistants made marks in note-books. The smell of onions again and the heat and sizzle that came off the stove as they were shifted around the pan with a wooden spoon. Men were clicking open cans of beer and popping the tops off bottles.

After the fight, it seemed, the crowd were going to make a day of it. Eat and drink and buy and sell. It was a fair, after all. Secret, free from taxation and rents and controls.

Men came over to Daddy and shook his hand. A man wearing a tweed jacket and a cloth cap slipped a fifty pound note into Daddy's hand. 'I've made a lot more from you today, I can tell you,' he said. He handed Daddy a bottle of beer and toasted him.

Someone brought out a bottle of whisky and someone else an unmarked bottle containing vodka from their own distillery. 'All above board, mind,' he said as he poured out some of the vodka into a plastic glass. 'And there's more of this in my van,' he said more loudly, so that others could hear. 'I'm selling it for five pound a bottle, over there in the blue Astra.'

As well as the fifty pound note, Daddy was offered other gifts. Tributes. A crate of cigarettes, crates of spirits, a lamb's carcass, skinned, wrapped and ready for Daddy to butcher. A box of vegetables. A box of kippers. Men had made money from Daddy today. I took the gifts and stowed them in the back of Ewart and Martha's car. Men patted me on the back, too, and they ruffled my hair as if I were a token of luck. They asked me to take sips from their drinks before they drank themselves like they were toasting Daddy through me. There were arms flung around me, and rough, male kisses applied to my forehead.

Where was Cathy?

The man in the tweed jacket and flat cap who had slipped Daddy a fifty walked over to me. 'You're a funny lad, aren't you?' He reached up to my hair, like the others, and rubbed and gently pinched my right cheek for good measure.

'Am I?'

'Aye, you are that. You're a funny little thing. A pretty little thing.' The man looked me up and down. 'Not built like your Daddy, are you?' He chuckled to himself. 'Are you going to be a boxer when you grow up?'

'No. I've never boxed. Daddy's never taught me.'

'Never taught you, eh? Funny for a boxing father not to pass it on to his son. It's a grand tradition, you know.'

He chewed on his lip and shuffled from side to side, then chuckled again.

I shrugged. 'Daddy dindt want it for me.'

'Is it that?' said the man. 'Or is it that you're not big enough? You've got skinny little arms, handt you? Not sure what weight class you'd be in but you've not got the muscle, have you? Tallish, mind, but skinny. Worst combination for a boxer that. You carry your weight in your height not your muscles. Worst build for a boxer.'

'Well it's fine by me.'

'Oh aye? Fine by you, is it? Well I woundt like sons who coundt hit back, that's for sure, no matter how pretty they were. It's true we can't all be like your Daddy, but I thought his own son would be something along the way to him.' He stopped for a moment. 'Aye, though,' he said. 'You are a pretty one.'

I had never thought of myself as pretty.

I thought about Vivien stroking my hair and my face in the way this man had.

Where was Cathy?

The man chuckled again as I walked away. Daddy was still occupied with his admirers.

I walked into the woods. The trees' trunks and enveloping foliage sheltered me from sounds of the fair, and I was left with my footsteps, the insects and the birds.

I walked in a straight line, following the rough path she had taken.

I had walked maybe 100 metres. Steps are slower in woodland.

'Daniel.' She was behind me with her back against a tree trunk. I had walked right past her without noticing. Her arms were crossed about her body.

'What you doing?'

'Nowt.' She did not meet my eyes.

'Daddy won.'

'I know.'

'Did you watch?'

'No.'

'Were you here?'

'Yes.'

'Could you hear from here?'

'No.'

'How then?'

'Because I knew he'd win. Dindt you?'

'Well yes, of course. I mean, of course. But I were nervous, I suppose.'

'I wandt.'

'Nothing is certain.'

'Yes it is. He is.'

She turned and walked away from me, through the trees, back to the clearing where the men had watched the fight. Some were moving on now. Clearing up, going home. I followed her. Skipped after her. My legs were as long as hers now but I still struggled to keep the pace. I never went anywhere or did anything with as much urgency as Cathy did. Big sister, little brother. I wanted her to always lead the way, tell me what was what, carry me home.

Chapter Eighteen

I woke suddenly; it was the middle of the night.
Dogs barked.

Our dogs.

I could hear their claws scratching at the rough
slate and their feet slipping as they tried to run.
More than once they slapped their heads against my
door as if searching for an open exit from a sinking
ship. I could hear them throw themselves at the walls
too. And at Cathy's door.

Daddy was up. I could hear his voice and the
raised voice of another man answering each other
across the threshold of our house.

'Bit funny indt it, don't you think?' the voice said.
'Bit of a funny coincidence?'

'I have no idea,' said Daddy. He was not entirely
calm.

'But you don't seem surprised. When you opened the door you seemed rather to have been expecting me.'

'Not really. Not expecting you. Unexpected visitors aren't unusual these days so I can't say I'm shocked when they turn up, even so early.'

'And you seemed to have been expecting this news.'

'No.'

The dogs were still scrabbling and barking, crashing intermittently against the walls. I strained to hear Daddy and the stranger over the din. I needed to be nearer to the door. I climbed out from beneath my covers. Away from my bed the air was thin and fresh. I had slept naked that night and my skin pinched itself back against the cold.

'Strangled, he was. His neck was so badly bruised we coundt tell if we'd cleaned off all the mud or not. My lad jus kept scrubbing away at him with soap and water to get all the marks off, like. I had to tell him to stop before he rubbed all his skin off too. And what I want to know is, who could do that? Who would have the strength? And who would want to? Motive, you see.'

'I think I can smell your meaning but I want you to speak to me directly. Ask me.'

'And it's a strange thing. A strange way to kill a man, even a boy. Round these parts men are shot or stabbed, or beaten so badly they die of their wounds.

Bleed slowly to death. They're not strangled, like. First off, it would take strength, like I said. He wandt small. Tall, strong lad he was. Played all those posh-boy sports up at his school. Rugger and that. Squash and what have you. He woundt have gone down without a fight. Not unless the man who did for him was exceptionally strong. Second, there's something so tender and sly about it. Why not keep your distance and clobber the man? Why not kick him when he's down? Why not stick a knife in him, or cleaner still a bullet so as you don't have to touch him at all. Why get up close and put your hands around his neck? Strange.'

The dogs were still moaning. Quieter now but keeping up the game. Setting each other off. Goading each other. Speaking to each other. Mimicking the conversation at the door.

'Was it by your hands, John?'

'You believe that it was.'

'I'm asking you. Now answer.'

'These hands did not throttle the boy.'

The dogs followed the silence of the men. I heard Daddy move to motion them out the front door then their paws pad and scrape on the slate then the gravel and earth, then fade as they followed his command and loped off down the hill.

'Do you believe me?'

'I do. But it don't matter what I believe. Their

blood is up, John. Price and his men. They've decided it were you, and they won't hear owt different.'

'What proof do they have?'

'None. And they won't get any. You know they won't involve the police. There won't be any kind of investigation. They'll just decide.'

'I know. I know the game. I know how it works around these parts.'

'You do. And you know they have a convincing story. The story's the thing.'

'The fight was won. I won Cathy and Danny's land for them. I had the paper in my hands. Signed by Price and me and the lawyer. It was witnessed. It was all secure. Why would I kill Price's boy now? Why would I disrupt everything like that?'

'Because—'

'Because what? Because I can't control myself? Because I'm little more than an animal?'

'Because of your daughter, John. Because they were seen together. Because the lad had been sniffing around her for months.'

Daddy was mute. I could feel him recoil, shift his weight, step back gently in surprise.

'What?'

'Were you blind to it? Such an attentive father, John, in so many ways yet you dindt see that?'

'What was there to see?'

'Him and her. Him mainly. Coming over to talk

to her whenever he could. But not in a friendly way. Not in a trying to get to know her kind of way. In a trying to get her away from the crowd kind of way. Sometimes his brother too. Him and his brother together. They were after her. Only she wandt keen, was she?'

'Of course she wandt.'

'No, no, she wandt.'

'She's too young.'

'Aye. And he's a creep. Both those lads are. Were, I should say. One's dead.'

'So they think I killed him for that?'

'But you dindt?'

'But I dindt.'

'But you would've? For that, I mean. If the lad had hurt her.'

'Of course.'

'There, then.'

'But I dindt.'

With no dogs to bark, when the men stopped speaking there was silence. I strained against the door frame, placing my ear canal exactly in line with the crack between the frame and the door, so as to hear them better should they start up again.

'They found the boy in the early hours. It was dark but they had his dogs with them. A couple of scent hounds, I don't know what sort, and they found him soon enough, darkness or no darkness. He was bundled up amongst the leaves with his coat laid over him like a shroud. Someone had laid it over his face, and I can see why: when we peeled it back his eyes were wide open, like they are sometimes, you know, on dead things. Animals, birds, people, the same. Wide open in astonishment; much wider than the eyelids could ever stretch in real life, like the lad wanted to capture all he could of the world, like he wanted to take a still image of that pretty little wood, the light coming through the trees, the little flowers beneath the ash and oaks, capture it and take it with him. Just that one still, wide-eyed picture. He used that last few seconds to fill his eyes with colour. But the colour from him had gone. And whatever shades he still held in his eyes, there were none in his skin. We knew he were dead right away. Wide, gaping eyes. Filthy, bruised and puckered neck. Scraps of brown leaves and moss in his mouth and stuck between his fine, white teeth. A dead man, no mistaking. Gorman was still there in the clearing. He'd stayed after the fight and the fair and after the carousing and after everyone else had left. He were sleeping overnight in the front of his van with the fish in their buckets and basins glugging around in the back. We lifted the lad between us. A long lanky thing, he was, but there were enough of us to manage. I took the middle part. I hoisted up his midriff while others took his head and feet. Damian wandt holding

237

the lad's head well enough. He had him more by the shoulders and his neck was bent back. I remember worrying that his bobbing head would snap his neck right through. Not that that can happen in that way but I remember worrying about it. And I were worried that that thick hair of his, longer now than when I last saw him, would get caught in the bracken as we cut a path for him back to the clearing. But we made it all right, and I reminded myself that dead things don't mind about a bit of hair pulling like the living would. And dead things don't worry like I do. Back in the clearing we found Gorman in his fish van and we rapped on the windows of the driving seat to wake him. Put him in the back of the van, we did. Back there with the barrels of living fish. Living, but all as cold as the dead boy. We laid him out in the centre with all the barrels of fish around him, like he was their dinner, laid out on a table in their midst for them to enjoy. I've seen a fully grown pike take a man's finger in its mouth and draw blood. Vicious creatures. So there he was. And we cleaned him up a bit before driving him back to the manor and his father. All we had was cold water in a bucket and an old bar of soap but my lad did the best job he could, scrubbing and scouring at his skin. Skin softer than any of us working men, softer than any fighting man. A gentlemen, in one sense. We got most of the dirt off him, and drove him to the manor with the fish slopping about in the back of the van. I can't deny he looked like his usual pretty self once he was clean. And when he saw his boy it was like Price was falling in love with him all over again, like he was seeing his beautiful son for the first time. I never thought he was a tender man, or that he could love like that. Men surprise you.'

Daddy spoke. 'He is a father like other fathers.'

'Quite. But his tenderness turned to anger soon enough, I can tell you that. His sorrow curdled. And now it's vengeance.'

'Aye.'

'Aye. He already has turned it on you. He already has his target. He was calling out your name like a baying buck. I believe you, John. You're a man of your word and you have no reason to lie to the likes of me. But if you think Price is going to talk it out you're mistaken. The only reason he's not up here already is because his men handt arrived at the manor yet. His thugs, I mean. The ones who'll be coming to collect you. He's sent for them and they'll come soon enough. Today, certainly. You'd be well advised not to be here. This is what I am trying to say to you, John. This is why I came up here. It was hard enough to slip away and Price will wonder where I've gone, but you're a good man. You're a good father and your children are sweet things. You must go. You and the kids must leave.'

'This is our home. It is our house and it is their land.'

'It doendt matter, John. Go. Go where he can't find you. That'll be far from here. What else can you do? You know very well that there's nothing you can do. You're the strongest man I have ever met. The strongest and the fastest and the cleverest man I have ever seen fight. But when ten men come here and point guns at your head your muscles don't count for a damn thing. Neither do your wits. There's nowt you can do at this point but run.'

Daddy made no answer. My breathing had quickened without me noticing and my heart was pounding in my chest. I was suddenly aware of the noises my body was making, of how loud my body had become. I wondered if the men could hear my heart and my lungs through the door of my room. I hoped not. They were too far away and too engrossed in their conversation and the wind they could hear outside would mask the sound of the air in me. But I felt like I could now hear the blood in my veins, coursing through the tiny channels like rushing white water in a gorge. I felt like I could hear it roiling inside of me, almost trying to cut new paths within me, larger channels to the sea outside. I had been prone to nosebleeds when I was a child. I put my right hand up to my face to check, almost instinctively. Usually I would smell the sweetness of the blood but there was nothing to smell or feel or taste. I was fine.

Daddy and the man at the door exchanged a few muffled words then the man left. A deep engine stumbled into life and hummed into the distance as the man drove away.

Daddy filled his own vast lungs with air then released it with a sound like the wind rushing between a pair of mountains.

'Daniel?' he said, quietly. Perhaps he had known I had been hiding there all along but he could not have been sure how much I had heard. I turned my door handle slowly, still trying to be quiet about it even though there was now no need. Daddy's was a dark silhouette in the dim hall light. The sun was still low in the sky and the edges of the trees outside were illuminated with bright precision.

I moved towards my father. 'Do you need to leave, Daddy?'

He shook his head. He took me in his arms for a moment and held me tight. He stooped to kiss my forehead and I felt for a moment his lips, so supple and surprisingly soft, and the bristles of his beard, at once silken and prickly. He took hold of my shoulders and turned me back towards my bedroom then placed a hand at the small of my back and gave me a little push.

'Sleep well, Danny. I will see you in the morning.'

V

I travel with Bill for days more. I am his company and he is mine. I am his succour. He is my warmth.

I search for her wherever we go. I search for her by the bus stations and by the railway tracks. I look at the adverts in shop windows. People with want for rooms, people with want for jobs. I do not have the courage to lose my faith. I bite at my fingernails as I stare out through the filthy panes of the lorry windows and scour the vertical and horizontal lines of concrete cityscapes for her familiar form.

Bill helps for a time, but finding my sister is not his main concern.

One night we take the lorry off the main roads, down some back lanes to spend the night in the quiet, away from the drill of rubber on tar. We jerk

then sway back from side to side as the weighty
wheels dip into deep potholes and fumble on the
rocks propped against the verge. There is no light.
Pitch dark. Few stars. No moon. An amber glow of
electricity far off. And then our own headlights. And
then a roe deer illuminated by our beacon. Caught.
Stopping short. Stood right there before us and star-
tled too, as we are. She is held as if preserved. As
if dead, stuffed, posed. Glass eyes sewn into place.
And what with her staring at us from behind glass,
behind the windscreen, it is as if she has been placed
in a museum with a natural habitat designed and
built and painted for her.

Bill jams his palm against the centre of the steering
wheel and the horn sounds like a hunting bugle and
the deer is gone and I hate him for it, the brute.

My Daddy would have done differently.

But then we stop in a lay-by. And I learn that a
body can mutate in the course of a night. And that
a night can bend with the curve of a body. He is
not so strong as he thinks. He is not so much of a
man. His voice is deep and his chest is broad and
there is more hair on his chin and jaw than on the
top of his head. But I have known others. I have
come from sterner stock.

I reach out to stroke him as he pulls at my jeans
but he bats away my hand. I do not mind. He is
nervous to the touch.

His weight is such that I am pinned. I notice the tattoos on his upper arms. They have faded and bled blues and greys against his blotchy skin. I make out the head of a serpent. There is an eagle caught in flight. Its talons and hooked beak are fierce. The body of a woman is stretched out along his forearm. Her breasts are bare.

He does not look me in the eye. We do not kiss. There is no conversation.

There is pleasure in the contact, if nothing else. In this brittle caress.

And in the morning I sit differently in my skin.

Chapter Nincteen

When you are terrified of everything nothing particularly afears. It was Cathy who first noticed the alteration. I had gone back to bed at Daddy's behest and had fallen asleep quickly. Cathy, who had slept through the night and through the arrival and departure of the man who had come to warn Daddy, was now up and thundering around our little cottage like a songbird that had flown through the window and was madly trying to retrace its path. The noise woke me but I did not get up and go to her. I remained tucked beneath my covers with my eyes closed, terrified. When she burst into my room she nearly lifted the door from its hinges. Its handle thudded against the wall and segments of roughly applied plaster crumbled to chalky dust.

'Wake up, Daniel, wake up,' she pleaded. I had never heard her plead.

I hesitated, wanting nothing less than to leave my safe, warm, bed. But she was my sister. And I knew instinctively, deeply, certainly, that something was very wrong.

I opened my eyes. 'I am awake,' I said. 'What is it?'

'Daddy's gone.'

'He must be in trees,' I replied immediately.

'I've been into the copse. He indt there. He indt in the house and he indt in the trees.'

'Did you go right to the heart of the copse? To the mother tree?'

'I've searched everywhere.'

I was silent, but this time through comprehension.

Cathy must have seen some understanding in my expression. 'Where is he? Where has he gone?'

'I don't know. I don't know for sure. He said he would stay, no matter what. And if he was going to leave, why did he leave without us?'

'Where has he gone?'

'I don't know. I said, I don't know.'

'What do you know?'

'I saw him early this morning. Just at dawn. A man came to the door and the dogs woke and then they woke me. They handt come back either. They must be out on the hill somewhere. Did they not wake you?'

'I slept right through the night. I was dreaming throughout. Dreaming dreams I don't remember.'

'I woke and I heard Daddy speaking with the man at the front door and snuck out of bed to listen. I dindt recognise the other man's voice. He wandt one of our lot and not someone from village. He came to warn Daddy. To warn him and to urge him to leave, get out of here, and—' I stopped. 'And to take us with him.'

'Why? We've won.'

'Because – and this is what the man said – because after the fight, in the middle of night, they found a body in woods behind the racecourse. A dead body. It was one of Price's sons.'

Cathy made no reaction, gave no sense that she had even heard or understood. She simply looked at me with those bright blue eyes, shining from that pale, lucid skin.

'The man told Daddy that Mr Price blamed him. Price and the others all think that Daddy killed son. I don't know which one it was. They had decided it must have been Daddy, from I don't know what, extent of strangulation, strength of hands that enclosed his neck and power of person behind them. They decided because of that and because, of course, Price hates him. His hatred of Daddy goes deeper than this recent trouble, I think, Cathy. It goes deeper than all this business about the fight and deeper than land on which we live. Stranger at door said Price had made up his mind it were Daddy killed his son, and now he's set on vengeance. There are no games any more. He's sending his men up, today, this morning perhaps, to get Daddy. To drag him back to them and do I don't know what. They woundt go to police, obviously.'

'Where is Daddy?'

'I told you I don't know. Stranger came up here to warn Daddy, like I said. He urged him to go but once he had left I came out. Daddy maybe knew I had been there, listening, the whole time. Daddy said he woundt go. He said—' But I struggled to remember what he had said.

'Of course he woundt. He would never leave us.'

I took my time to think this through, before I replied. 'I know that,' I said. 'I do.' I stopped speaking for a moment and bit my lip. 'But where is he?'

We took the back road to the village. The pavement leading to Ewart and Martha and their house and garden was sticky with three days of heat. A thin film of condensation, which had sat thick in the air, had dropped and compacted on the tarmac. It was slick.

I had persuaded Cathy to follow me here. She had been unsure.

We knocked the door not once but twice. The first time, I rapped my knuckles gently against the pane of stained glass at the centre of the door. The second time Cathy thumped the wood.

It swung open. Ewart and Martha stood at the threshold, both. Both, husband and wife, held a strange countenance and a skewed stance. They looked between us, my sister and I. They looked above us and around us. They looked behind them into their own home.

I ventured. 'Have you seen our Daddy?'

Martha glanced at Ewart. Ewart held my gaze.

'That's a fine thing,' he said.

I made no reply.

'That's a fine thing,' he said again.

'I'm sorry,' I said. 'What's a fine thing?'

He held me still, with his eyes that is, for a moment more.

'You two coming here, looking for your Daddy, looking for him. That, I tell you, is fine.'

But he did not mean fine like I mean fine or Cathy or Daddy mean fine when it is a fine day or when you ask for something reasonable and they tell you it is fine.

'Ewart, love,' said Martha, 'it's hardly their fault. They can hardly be blamed. For any of it.'

'No? They're old enough, aren't they? They're old enough to participate in the business end of things, why not in this? They're a tight family, this lot, that's what they always said. That's why we took to them. You know as well as I, Martha, that we would never have trusted a man like John, man with his reputation, and let him into our home and into our confidences if it handt been for these two. A father with children is a much more reliable prospect than a single, lone man. It's all about perception. That's how these tricksters lure you in, see. Come with a family and you're trustworthy. They're probably all in on it. What have you two come for, then, my wife's jewellery? The car?'

'Enough,' demanded Martha. 'They came to see where their father is, and they thought he might be here. They're at as much of a loss as we are. They had nothing to do with any of it.'

'Nothing to do with any of what?' asked Cathy.

'Perhaps you'd best come in,' said Martha.

'Perhaps they had better not!'

Ewart put an arm across the threshold to bar our entrance. Neither Cathy nor I had made any moves to enter.

'You could just tell us while we wait here,' I suggested.

Martha took a deep, leaden breath. 'Your father came here first thing. At dawn, or just after, even. Neither Ewart nor I were up, but we heard him at the door.'

'That we did. We were happy to see him. It was early but he always did keep irregular hours. We were used to welcoming him into our homes at all times of the day and night. Trusting fools that we are.'

'Enough, Ewart. It's your pride. It's your pride.'

'It's more than my pride. It's fifty thousand pounds, Martha. Money that wasn't even ours.'

'I know that. I know that. But these two children need to know.'

Ewart took a step back and folded his arms over his belly. He couldn't look at us.

'He came round here before dawn,' said Martha again. 'Your daddy. He asked to come in, and, of course, we welcomed him. He said he had need to see the books. The one where we recorded all the business. All that's been going on these last months. Well we kept all that in a safe upstairs, all the names and the money they'd been giving us. Because you know there were dues. Union dues, I suppose. Well, those involved, as you may know, were paying their rent money for each week or month to us. To me and Ewart. Just for safe keeping. For if the strike went tits up. Or for if we came to the kind of agreement where the landlords submitted to our demands and in return they got the withheld money back, in whole or in part. And, well, that's what we agreed to, isn't it. Your Daddy settled his score with the land for the house in that fight. Price had wanted him to fight for him all along. You two have no idea how much money was riding on that fight, and how much Mr Price stood to gain from John cooperating with him again, fighting for him, like he used to. But separate to all that was the deal we struck with all the landlords collectively. Mr Price, yes, but the others too. And not about your house and land but that of all those in the rented houses and flats, the old council properties. They agreed to a rent freeze. They agreed to a more reasonable rent for those who quite clearly could not afford. They agreed to forget about arrears. And they agreed to fix some of the things that had broken. Not all, mind, we asked people to take care of some of their own stuff too, and people from the community who are good at that sort of thing, but the landlords agreed to do a lot. And we would pay back the money that had been withheld. Not at first, but after we saw that they would keep their word. And, of course, there was something of your Daddy's fight in that. It sealed the promise. Sealed it in blood. Don't ask me how. But it did. Only the money, near fifty thousand pounds, given to us by all those good folk who trusted us and expected us to see them right, it's gone. Your Daddy went upstairs to see the books – we trusted him with the key to the safe – and he rustled away the money. All of it. And then he left.'

Ewart took up the tack. 'And as the morning wore on we heard stories. Stories on which you two might be able to expand. Stories from Peter down the way and others in the village. A story about a dead boy in the woods. That son of Price's. The pretty one. The prettier one. Dead. Strangled. And his watch and money robbed.'

'His watch and money robbed?' asked Cathy.

'Aye. Your Daddy clearly wandt content with all he had won that day. Or else his blood was up. Clearly there's no satisfying men like your Daddy when their blood is up. When they're in the mood for violence. When that violence is the violence of avarice. They'll go to the lowest possible limits of greed and thuggery. I should have known. I was a fool. I should have known. A man like that. With his reputation. Mr Price is a wrong'un, to be sure, but his boy was just a boy. Just a lad. And his neck was nearly clean snapped by all accounts, such was the force with which your Daddy gripped it.'

'It's not true,' said Cathy, quietly.

'Not true, is it?' said Ewart. 'You dare to defend him? That's fine. That's fine.'

Again, he did not really mean fine. He meant rich, that's rich. Or he meant, that is absurd, or he meant, that is offensive to me and to everything I stand for.

'You've just assumed,' said Cathy. 'Yesterday you

were his friend, you were cheering for him with the others, but today you accuse him.'

'He stole fifty thousand pounds from me!'

'So you accuse him of strangling Charlie Price. There is nothing to suggest it were him. Only rumours. And only rumours that tell you he was motivated by greed, that he stole from Charlie Price. You believe that he stole the wallet and the watch because you believe he stole fifty thousand pounds from the safe in your house.'

'He did steal fifty thousand pounds from the safe in my house!'

'But he dindt kill Charlie Price. I did.'

Ewart and Martha stood in silence. I stood in silence. Cathy was silent too.

Then, after some time, Ewart spoke. 'You're a little girl, Cathy. You might think you're big and tough like your daddy, but you're a wee girl. Don't play games with us.'

'I'm not playing games with you.'

'Perhaps you're trying to protect your father,' said Martha. 'That's good of you, really it is, but it's not helpful here.'

'I'm not trying to be helpful. I'm trying to tell the truth. I killed Charlie Price.'

'Cathy.'

'I killed Charlie Price. I strangled the life out of him. I am glad I did it and I would do it again.'

Martha and Ewart Royce said nothing. They looked at Cathy, aghast. Martha took hold of the wooden door and slammed it shut. The glass pane rattled.

Cathy and I stood for a few moments more, turned and walked back down the garden path.

I did not ask any more of Cathy. I did not ask questions nor request that she repeat what she had said.

We walked along a couple of streets and still said nothing. We split up and agreed to meet back at home in an hour. Cathy went to Peter's and to some of the others we knew from the village. I made towards Vivien's house on the outskirts, past the common land, past the stray, back towards where we lived, me, Cathy and Daddy. Cathy had not wanted to come to Vivien's house. She had said she would rather speak with the honest people of the village. So I walked down the lane alone.

The curtains were drawn, not just the upstairs windows but the downstairs windows too.

I knocked on the door. There was no answer and no sounds from within.

I knocked again. No answer. No hushed voices. No bustle of cooking or cleaning. No radio.

I waited, and knocked, and thumped, and waited. I paced the front garden. There was no answer yet I knew that she was at home. I knocked, I waited,

I struck the door with both fists. Once. Twice. I waited.

With each passing minute I knew more fervently that Vivien was truly inside, hiding from me, listening to me knock and thump, perhaps watching me through a slit in the curtains, watching me pace, watching my skin flush, watching tears well in my eyes.

I had come to depend on Vivien with a weight I could only just acknowledge, now, as I set that weight down. Daddy had built me a home – for me and for him and for Cathy. He had built shelter, arranged wood and stone over our heads in such a way that kept off the wind and the snow and the rain. He had given us safety and warmth. But, for me, in a way that I could not quite fathom let alone describe, Vivien had built a home for me too. A nest. It was a different kind from the one by the copse on the top of the hill. There was nothing tangible about the home I felt in Vivien. There were no bricks, no mortar, no rivets, no joints. It kept off no weather. It sank slowly into no mud. But it had a kind of hearth and a kind of fire. It was a place with a future. A place of possibility.

'Vivien!' I shouted. I knocked again. And waited. 'Vivien!'

There was no use in it. I gave up. I turned for the last time and walked back down the path towards the gate and the lane that led home.

As I turned onto the track, Vivien's front door was flung open, and the woman who I had met the year before, so composed, ran from her house towards me. Unkempt hair was tossed by a sudden gust. Her eyes were red.

'If you want to talk, Daniel, you'd better come in!'

At first I remained motionless. I stood for a while to take in the scene. Then I followed her inside and she shut the door, but we didn't make it past the hall. 'He's gone, Daniel. And no, I don't know where. That he wouldn't say.'

'But he came to see you.'

'Yes, he did. You've only missed him by half an hour or so.'

'I should have come here first. I knew I should have come here first. But that means he might still be near.'

'You won't find him. When he moves, he moves quickly. And he doesn't want you to chase him.'

'He said he would stay.'

'How could he. There are men after him. Men and dogs. Men that want to kill him. Really kill him, this time. Catch him alive, if possible, drag him back to Price and kill him slowly. This isn't business, any more, he killed that boy.'

'He dindt,' I said.

'Of course he did.'

257

'Is that what he said? Is that what he told you?'

'Well, he didn't deny it.'

'But did he tell you that, really? Did you ask him directly and did he tell you directly?'

'He didn't have to. Word spreads fast. I had a phone call from Ewart first thing this morning. He wanted to warn me. He said that your Daddy had killed the Price boy, strangled him to death, nearly took his head off with the force of his fists, then he'd gone to Ewart and Martha's at dawn and stolen some money.'

'But still you let him in when he came?'

'Well, your father had always been wild. I always knew he was no angel.'

'That's true,' I said. 'But he dindt kill Charlie Price.'

'Whatever he did. Whatever he did or didn't do, Price's men are certain. They found your Daddy's coat draped over the boy's body, you know? Like a blanket. Like a shroud.'

'I believe you.'

'John's a marked man. If they catch him, there's no telling what they'll do to him. I know he's tough. We all know that. But this is different. Running was the only chance he had.'

I nodded. 'Perhaps.'

I looked through an open door into the front room.

Vivien did not invite me further into the house. It was cold to me.

'Did he come here to say goodbye to you?' I asked.

'In part.'

'What was the other part?'

'He asked me—' She stopped speaking.

'He asked you what?'

'It was a big ask. Beyond what most people would ask of each other.'

'What did he ask you?'

'I don't know if I should say.'

'Vivien! My father disappeared from me this morning and there are men and dogs hunting him, to kill! Tell me!'

'He wanted you and Cathy to come here. He wanted me to look after you for a little while until he could find somewhere safe. Then he would come and get you.'

I did not say anything just then. I wanted her to finish.

'Only it's a lot to ask,' she continued. 'I've got my own life, and yes I feel sorry for you, but it's a lot. And besides, you and Cathy are fairly self-sufficient. You two wouldn't want to move in here with me. You're your own family. You've got each other. And I'm not one to share my space. I'm too old and too used to living alone, now. Perhaps years ago it would have worked. There was a time in my life when it might have been a lovely thing. But not now. It's too late.'

'Daddy asked you to do that?'

'Yes, he asked that.'

I thought about it for a moment. A scene in which somebody who is running for their life asks an old friend to care for their children, and that old friend refuses. 'Well,' I said. 'I suppose you're right. Cathy and I can make do at the house.'

'That's what I thought. You be careful though.'

She seemed to want me to leave.

'Yes,' I said. 'Yes, we will.'

'Because Price and his men might come for you, you see. To get to Daddy.'

'I suppose they might.'

'So don't open the door to any strangers.'

'No,' I said. 'We won't.'

I took a step back. 'Thank you for letting me in.'

For a moment she had forgotten that initially she had not. She looked taken aback. 'Oh, no, I mean, of course. Of course I was going to let you in. I was upstairs with the vacuum on, that's all. You're always welcome here. To visit.'

'Thank you, that's kind.'

I opened the front door and stepped out into the sun. I closed the door behind myself, thinking that the right thing to do but it was stiff in its frame and

I had to shunt it a couple of times, and Vivien, saying something muffled that I did not hear, pushed it from within.

The walk home was slow.

We hid in the trees when Pricc's men came to search the house. It was mid-morning and we heard the dirty, claggy exhausts of their vans long before they got to the top of our hill. Cathy suggested that we stay in the house and confront them. She said we should show them we were not cowards. I persuaded her to leave off on this idea and instead we let ourselves out the back and ducked and skipped as quietly as we could until we hit the cover of the copse. There was no sign of Jess or Becky. I looked for them out on the horizon as we skulked across the open ground but caught no sight.

The soft, wet moss on the woodland floor and the sallow bark of the ash smelt more familiar this morning than ever before. Birds in the branches and the small mammals in the undergrowth kept the silence with us, though I saw shining eyes and flickering indigo feathers through apertures in the leaves.

I breathed slowly and deliberately and felt Cathy do the same. The vans parked on the stony earth outside our front door, and the men in the front seats got out. One rushed to the back to unstick the big double doors of both vehicles and five men climbed from the galley of each. Fourteen there were in total. I squinted to see if any were recognisable, feeling sick at the thought that it might be anyone we knew here, and, clearly, something had shifted. At least four were farm labourers who had come up to our bonfire on that night, weeks ago now. And all the men looked set on work like they were climbing out of the backs of vans to pick strawberries or sort potatoes. A couple even had spades, though to be put to a different use. Others gripped baseball bats and crowbars.

The men started circling the house. No one wanted to knock on the front door but a few – the bravest – went up to the windows, stuck an eyeball against the glass and shielded it from glare with a cupped hand. They paced for the best part of a minute before a smallish man with bulldog shoulders shuffled his crowbar to his right hand then swung it at the door, by way of a knock. I heard the sound briefly resonate within the house, like he had thumped an empty oil-drum.

'Open up, John! You know why we're here!' the man called.

Of course there was no answer. Daddy, as we knew, was not there.

'Open up, John!' called another from behind the bulldog man, encouraged by his companion's engagement. His accent was from north of here: still England but near the Scottish border.

Taking courage, the other men came closer to the house and some started beating on the walls and windows. A pane of glass smashed as one man tapped it too hard with his bat. He jumped back from the scene, shocked. Everybody was on edge. I could feel it.

A man in a grey tracksuit with soft blonde hair and a mawkish face, who could not have been much older than Cathy, went over to the man with bulldog shoulders, who appeared to be in charge. 'I don't think he's in, Doug,' said the mawkish man.

'Not answering his door more like. Holed up inside there with the kids, he is.'

'None of us can see owt through the windows. There's no sign of them.'

'So you want us to just leave it, do you?'

'That's not what I'm saying.'

'You want us to go back to Price empty-handed. Do you think that'll go well for us?'

'That's not what I'm saying. If they're not there, there's nowt we can do, is what I'm saying.'

'We better check,' another man called from around the other side of the house. I could not see him, only hear his voice.

'That's right,' said the man with bulldog shoulders. 'We'd better check.'

He went back to the front door and started beating at the lock with his crowbar. Others went to the windows and smashed the glass, deliberately this time. I became aware of Cathy at my side. She was flexing the muscles in her arms and thighs as if ready to leap but her fists were clenched tight around the uncovered roots of a large ash, holding her to the ground. Impetuous as she was, at least she had the sense not to run at them. I considered doing something small to reassure her – to remind her that I was still there. My right hand hovered for a moment at the crook of her elbow but I thought better of it. Her whole body was held taut like a hunting trap, and any touch, no matter how slight, might set her off. We had to wait it out.

Our front door was made of oak and it held fast even when attacked at its weakest point. He tried the corners, but still it held. Had Cathy and I been inside we could have locked the extra bolts that Daddy had fitted – for situations like this, no doubt – but as it was, the single lock, fixed from the outside, was enough.

Until they brought out the battering ram, that was. Police issue, by the look of it. Wielded by four men, the door frame came away from the wall and fell to the floor with a single, ponderous thud. The wood was too heavy to bounce. And then they were inside, and we could no longer see them apart from the two stationed at the door, keeping watch.

We heard them well enough. They set about tearing up our things and smashing furniture, some of which I had made with my own two hands.

Cathy remained as she was, poised. But I turned away, confident that they would not hear the under-growth rustle as I turned my back on them and sat in the moss looking instead into the depths of the copse.

I do not know how long the men stayed inside destroying our things and ripping at the guts of our house but they were quiet when they had finished. A job well done. They came outside and lingered only to catch their breaths before filtering back into the two vans. One started up and accelerated imme-diately but paused when the driver saw he was not being followed by the other vehicle. A head was poked out the window to check on the situation but he must have been waved on by the driver of the second van because he soon tucked himself back into his cabin and started up again. As the first van sped out of sight, the driver of the second got out, walked around to the front and opened up the bonnet. There was a problem with the engine. I could smell it now: a faint dark smoke had drifted towards us in the trees and had just now reached my nostrils. Burnt oil. As he worked at the engine Cathy kept her eyes fixed upon him like a lion in the scrub watching gazelle.

I was looking out towards the house when I heard the strike at Cathy's head. It was an unfamiliar sound and so close, simultaneously soft and chafing like a football bouncing on gravel. Then Cathy's head was in the dirt. I looked down and saw her: I did not look up to see the man who had struck her. She coughed into the loose soil and it kicked back a cloud of umber. She was not unconscious but, a moment later, I was.

Chapter Twenty

I woke in her arms. Cathy had placed my head on her lap and she was cradling it. I felt something cold and wet on my forehead. She mopped my brow with a towel then my cheeks and lips. She had lifted a bottle of water and, seeing that my eyes had opened, she raised my head, put the bottle to my mouth and urged me to drink. The shock of the cold water made my head feel worse but I soon discovered how thirsty I had been. Feeling well enough to raise my arm, I took the bottle myself and finished it then considered that I should have perhaps left some for her.

'I've already drunk,' she said, reading my thoughts. 'You're fine.'

My head was far from fine. I did not need to

touch it to check for blood. I could smell it on my face.

'They got us, then,' I said.

'Looks like it.'

'Where are we?'

'They put us in a van and brought us out to a farm. Mr Price's, I think. They locked us in a shed round the back of the house, near a big barn. I was awake the whole time. You were out cold.'

I shuffled my body into a more comfortable position.

'There's a load of them,' she said. 'Too many for Daddy. Perhaps.'

'Is Daddy here?' I asked.

'Not yet.' Cathy was still holding her hope out in front of her for all the world to see. I had swallowed mine.

I looked around. The shed would have been completely dark but for a thin row of windows just beneath the corrugated iron roof. There were shelves containing stacks of cardboard boxes, canisters and plastic bottles. Garden twine, sheets of bubble wrap, pull-ties, paraffin. That sort of thing. The floor was mucky and covered with pelts of green AstroTurf, which were mucky too. In one corner there was a table laden with nursery plants, little shoots of something or other poking out of their individual black pots.

'Did you kill that boy, Cathy?'

She had been busy rearranging the folds and creases in her jeans and did not look across. We were sat right next to each other on the mucky floor and I could hear her halt her breath but she did not look across.

'I don't mind if you did,' I continued. 'It's nowt to me. You're my sister and I love you. I have believed everything you've ever said and I will believe everything you ever will say. And if you did it there was reason, even if that reason was just that you wanted to. It's nowt to me. You're my sister.'

She still did not look across. Nor did she speak. I put my hand around her shoulder.

'There was nowt else I could do,' said Cathy. 'I wandt strong enough to just push him off. If I'd fought him just to put him down on the ground long enough that I could get away, he would have just got straight back up and caught me again. He was so much bigger than me. So much stronger. If I had fought by any kind of rules I would've lost. It's just like Daddy's always said. If I'd slapped him round the face or punched him he would have slapped and punched me harder. If I'd grappled with him, he would have had me. Of course he would have. That's the way it goes. He's a boy, growing into a man, and I'm a girl, growing into a woman. The only thing I could do was to pretend – for just a moment – that

that's not how the game is played. You woundt understand.'

'I would. I do. Please tell me.'

'I just. I just knew that the only way I could regain
any kind of control over it all – over myself, my
body, the situation – was if that control was complete.
My action had to outweigh anything he might do
by such a long way that he woundt even have the
chance to act. Because, with the way things were set
up between us, he had many chances; I had one. So
I took it. It was like everything inside me came
together in one moment to a single point and that
point was my clasped grip around his throat. I held
him like that, tightly, for minutes and minutes. Long
after he was dead. I had to make sure. Like I said,
I had one chance.'

'I didn't even know he was there at the racecourse,'
I said. 'Either of Mr Price's sons. I handt thought
on him much since all this, not since they came to
see us that time, and I took them around the copse.'

'I suppose you woundt. I dindt say anything about
it and there's been other things to think about. He'd
been having a go for a while though. You know I
dindt like staying at Vivien's for her lessons so I used
to go outside and go round about. I'd go for walks
and sometimes just sit beneath a tree or whatever
or I'd go and see if I could spot some birds. Just to
occupy myself, you know. I were never much into

270

what you and Vivien like. Reading and that. So that's what I did. Although I'd find myself interrupted by those lads, Tom and Charlie. It happened once that they were out with their dogs and guns and the dogs found me lying on my stomach by a fox den, waiting to see the kits. I'd been going to that spot for a few days, after I'd seen where the den was and that the fox – the dog fox – was going back and forth with food, like it would if it was bringing it home for a suckling vixen. I'd been waiting there for the last few days for the chance of seeing something. And then I heard the hounds howling, coming towards me. I thought they'd got the scent of the foxes, maybe they had, they would have flushed it for the lads to shoot. But then they got my scent and came at me and I jumped up from the grass and Tom had his gun pointed in my direction. I thought he were going to shoot. Maybe that's what he wanted me to think. And the dogs were all yapping and sniffing round me like it was my scent they'd been given all along. Tom lowered his gun and they came forward. They wanted a chat, they said. I gave them what they wanted, answered their stupid questions, laughed at their stupid jokes. Then I told them after a while that I had to get home and they seemed okay with that. Only they found me again a few days later. And then again.'

Cathy was hunched over her knees. She rested her

chin on one and put her hands on her shoes to play with the laces. 'And well,' she said, 'that's how it went.'

'Why dindt you say owt to Daddy?'

'Because it were my thing. It were my problem to deal with. I can't always go to Daddy whenever anything happens. I have to be able to deal with things by myself.'

'But not this.'

'Yes this. Yes this. This were my part of it. Daddy had other stuff to deal with. Daddy and Ewart and the others had to do what they were doing. The Prices were coming at us from all sides and this was my part. And Daddy won't always be around. And even if he is, it is my life and my body and I can't stand the thought of going out into the world and being terrified by it all, all o' the time. Because I am, Danny, I am. And I don't want to be. I don't want to feel afraid. All I kept thinking about was Jessica Harman, thrown into that canal, and all those other women on the TV, in newspapers, found naked, covered in mud, covered in blood, blue, twisted, found in the woods, found in ditches, never found. Sometimes I can't stop thinking about them. Sometimes I can't stop thinking about how I'm turning into one of them. I'm older now and soon my body will be like theirs. I dindt want to end up in a ditch. I dindt want that any more than you want to be a fighting man like

Daddy, or a labouring man, out sorting potatoes on a farm all day until your limbs get caught and broken and chopped in the dirty machinery, dirty iron and dirty steel. We all grow into our coffins, Danny. And I saw myself growing into mine.'

I took hold of my sister's hand. The light seeping into our jail from the high windows darkened as she spoke, filtered by a sombre parade of ashen clouds. It had been hot for days. Hot and humid and dense and now the engulfing heavens were trapping the heat within like the stone lid over a sarcophagus.

Chapter Twenty-One

We remained in the shed for at least a day, a night, and another day, but we slept for much of it, curled together like caterpillar and leaf. Food was brought. Bread and jam at breakfast, a couple of microwave pizzas in the evening. We had not eaten anything like it for months, not since school dinners. I was not used to so much white bread. My insides ached. And they were tight with nerves.

Neither of us recognised the men who brought the food. They were different each time. They shuffled in, placed the tray down, then they left. I looked behind them through the opened door to the outside on each occasion but noted nothing. Each vista was a quiet simulacrum of the last: duller, hazier, but no significant alterations. From these brief glimpses of outside I could gauge no movement, no changes to provoke either concern nor hope.

In the evening of the second day, three men came to the shed. The bolts were shunted open and the key turned in the lock. They waited outside.

'You're to come,' said one. He stood in the middle, slightly forward of the other two.

'Where are we going?' asked Cathy.

'You're to come, that's all. You'll find out soon enough, young lady.'

Neither Cathy nor I moved.

'You'll be coming either way,' said the man. He was trying to menace but it was clear he had no real power. Such things can easily be discerned from very little contact. The merest waver in a man's voice, the smallest declination of the eyes to the floor, a look of minute sympathy. He said, 'You'll be coming the easy way or the hard way.'

'Right. Yeah. Well. You could just tell us where we're going then we'd probably come, woundt we?'

The man in the middle looked to either side for support. One of them shrugged. The other just stared at Cathy.

'We're taking you up to see Mr Price.'

'Right then,' said Cathy. 'In that case, we're definitely coming.' She got up and I followed. 'Was that the easy way?' she asked as we stepped across the threshold.

275

He might have given her a clip round the ear but I could tell he was afraid. She was nothing to him in size, of course, but my sister always had a certain manner. There's power in the truth. In saying what you really mean. In being direct.

We walked with the three men through the back garden. There were further outhouses, a network, for tools, for boots, for guns. We weaved through vegetable patches and greenhouses, other potting sheds. The men did not lead us into the house but around it, on a thin gravel path that skirted the outer wall. We came to the front of the house and to an oval forecourt that stood before the steps up to the grand double front doors. Seven or eight vehicles, of different sorts, were parked around. I recognised Mr Price's Land Rover, and his Jaguar. There were the Transit vans, and also a pick-up truck with a dirty tarpaulin flung over something bulky in the back.

Another group of men, possibly fifteen, were huddled. Hands in the pockets of dark jackets, all. Mr Price was among them, centred, gazing out towards the perimeter of his property, where an emerald hedge stood high.

The doors of the van we had come down in were open. Its engine was choking. The air around was black with exhaust. The stench hit my nostrils.

Mr Price glanced over at us and quickly away. His face looked hard worn, steadfast.

We were led to the van and bundled in the back.

'What's going on?' I asked. 'Where're you taking us?'

'Up back to yours, via a stop on the way,' said the man.

'Back to ours?'

'We've found your Daddy.' He winked and grinned with teeth then slammed the van door tight shut, soaking us in a stiff darkness.

Cathy, with a sudden panic, ran to the door and rattled the steel with her fists. 'Let us out!' She hammered. 'Let us out!'

I remained where I was, and held firm to the side of the van. The choking engine spluttered and caught and the van rolled then jolted then accelerated sharp. Cathy fell back and winded herself. I held on but grazed my elbow on something sharp. I felt a moisture in the crook of my right arm. It could have been blood or it could have been sweat. It was too dark to see.

Cathy coughed and caught her breath as the van hurtled forwards. I shuffled my feet apart to balance as the floor rattled beneath us. The roads and lanes round here were rutted after years of frosts and thaws and disrepair. I thought I heard dogs howling in the distance. They could have been ours. I had not seen Jess and Becky since they had run out of the house and down the hill. They often went roaming round about, but usually they found their way home.

We had not gone all that far when the van shuddered to a halt. Men leapt out. Shouting. Doors slammed. The sound of men running on grass and tarmac and gravel.

Cathy crawled to the door of the van where there was a slight crack in the rubber seal. She angled her nose against the metal in such a way that her eye was more or less aligned with the crack.

'Can you see much?' I whispered.

She rearranged her body, tilted her head, and looked out again.

'I don't recognise the place.'

There was more shouting. No words clear enough to make out. But there was much in the tone. An anger. A brutal excitement.

Cathy shuffled away from the door and sat. I could see her outline, dimly. It was too dark to see features or expression but I knew her well enough to recognise when she was afraid. Her ribs shuddered as she breathed. She was still such a little thing.

'I don't feel good about this, Daniel. If you get the chance to get out of this, take it. Go, run, and don't look back.'

'I woundt leave you.'

'But that's just what I mean. Do. Do leave me. I need you to know that I'll be fine. No matter what they do to me, what happens to me. I'll be fine. In my self, I mean. They can do their worst and I promise you I'll go somewhere else in my mind's eye, for as long as I need to, and I'll be fine. An experience is what you make of it. If you tell yourself that it means nothing, then that's exactly what it means. So you just run. Promise me.'

'I don't want to promise that.'

'Please. I can look after myself, in the only way I know how. And the thought of something happening to you is far worse for me than the prospect of something happening to me. I mean that. I would worry so much. I would never get over it. But if something happens to my body. Well, I am able to put myself in such a position that it's like it's not really happening. And if it's like it's not really happening that means it's not really happening. Do you see what I mean?'

I told her that I did not.

'Well. Never mind. Just promise me you'll run when I need you to run. I will be safer and better equipped if you run. If I know you're safe and out of it.'

I said nothing for a long while. The shouting and running had stopped. There was an unnerving silence. I moved over to sit by Cathy and took her hand as I had back in the shed.

'If we're off to meet up with Daddy,' I said, 'I'm sure we'll be all right.'

Cathy squeezed my hand, weakly.

'Promise you'll run,' she said.

'I promise.'

The van accelerated once again and Cathy and I rocked back and forth as the way became rough. Then, all of a sudden, we slid to the back. The front of the vehicle had lifted. We were climbing a steep hill. The hill was ours. Perhaps I could tell from the precise undulations in the track. Perhaps I could smell something of home.

The van stopped and the driver stepped out and walked round to the back. He opened the double doors. Dusk had come and gone and we found ourselves looking out into the night. By starlight and moonlight I recognised the three men that had collected us before. Cathy and I rose.

She whispered to me, 'Do as I say. We'll get out with them, we'll comply, and they won't manhandle us. Then when I say, you run.'

We stepped out.

The men flanked us but did not seize us.

We began to walk towards the house.

'Daniel,' said Cathy, aloud. She meant for me to go. But I remained. 'Daniel,' she said again.

We were walking with the men towards our own front door.

'Daniel,' said Cathy.

I continued to walk. I was behind her, with two men at either side and one in front, leading the way.

We were nearly inside. The copse was to my right

and, beyond, the shaded hills then the flats of the levels.

'Daniel, run!' Cathy shouted, frustrated that I was not moving to her command.

I remained where I was. One of the men chuckled, then, of a sudden, he took Cathy roughly by her arms, pinned them behind her body at such an angle that only the shoulders and elbows of a supple and lanky young girl could stand.

It was not the worst thing they could have done, to be sure, yet it hurt her. She moaned, though she did not shriek.

'Don't be a damn fool, love,' said the man who had laughed and grabbed.

With that, I got shoved from behind through the space where the front door had been. These men were full-grown men. These men were strong, burly, full-grown men employed for the purpose of doing harm. They were tough. With but a light push I was half-winded.

We were marched into the kitchen. I stepped on broken glass. The windows had been shattered and cupboards were open with their contents strewn. Two of the chairs I had lovingly crafted with the help of my father had been smashed. The legs of the kitchen table, chopped roughly, lay on the floor at the sides of the room. The top, the long, thick oak board, was absent.

281

They bundled us in. They were more ragged in their movements than they had been. Rougher, more unkind. They took us to the sides of the room and held us, firm. Another of the men gripped me as the first gripped Cathy. My bony arms were held tight behind my back by the elbows. I was young and thin and flexible too but my shoulders ached, and my ribs where they were squeezed, and the skin at the crook of my arm where the man pinched it with his leathery palms and annealed knuckles. I yelped.

For Cathy the initial pain had passed but her breathing deepened as her body found a way through the discomfort.

Other men filed into the room. They thumped each other on the arms and nodded. There was brief, clipped chatter. Cathy and I were shovelled to the sides, still held tight.

And then hush.

Into the room, into our kitchen, walked Mr Price. Like it was his own. His parlour. His workshop. His counting house. Like we were spiders climbing on his walls. Slugs suckered to his window, peering in.

His face showed wear. He was gaunt. But there was something human. A man whose son had been strangled to death in the woods, not a couple of nights before.

Tom Price, the elder of the two lads, walked behind

him. He looked in horror and choler at my sister and I as our bodies were bent by the fists of others.

Father and son arranged themselves in a corner of the room. Mr Price did not direct his gaze at us. Not once. He stared above our heads and above the heads of the men he had hired. His jaw was locked, and it held the rest of his face in stiff composure.

The space was almost full with men at each side, sitting up on the work surfaces, tucked into corners and squeezed against the sides. Only the wall nearest the door was vacant, deliberately so, as men pushed and shoved into all the other spaces.

The silence remained. It was held by Mr Price. His presence settled others with a quiet trepidation. He surveyed.

A moan was heard outside. And it was as if the silence deepened. Everyone heard it. Then a sickening bellow. And something heavy dragging. And the voices of other men struggling to move an object.

'Push. Push. I'll guide him in.' The words were muffled, heard through two shut doors and a whirling wind.

'The corner's got stuck on this clump of turf.'

The other man's response did not make it into the room but was carried away by a sudden gust. They continued to drag whatever they were dragging. Step by step. Push and pull. It scraped and thudded. All eyes were on the door. Another moan was heard.

A distinctive moan from distinctive vocal chords.

I couldn't help it. I called out. 'Daddy! Daddy!' I shouted.

'Somebody shut that boy up,' snapped Mr Price from the corner. He did not look over. He hardly moved his lips as he issued the command.

The man holding me removed one of his fists from my arms and smacked my lower jaw. I tasted blood and with my tongue felt something loose. He shook me for good measure, bound my arms up in his own and pushed down so I had to lean forward and bend my knees.

I panted with the pain. I fiddled with the loose molar. I tasted blood. I fiddled some more with the tooth. I paid attention to this object in my mouth, to the feeling of its rough top as my tongue rubbed against it, and the feeling of the soft, tenderised gum beneath.

The door was opening. The man who had been doing the dragging could just about be seen, his back turned as he attended to his burden.

I concentrated on finding with my tongue the place in my mouth from where the blood was coming in. I fiddled around with the tooth. I enjoyed the distraction of the sharpness.

The man had now backed fully into the room. He was assisted by three others in his task. They held a board of wood. It was the top of our oak table. I saw where the legs had been and how roughly and carelessly they had been hacked off. The men carrying the table top now held it by these stubs.

I fiddled with my tooth. My back was bent in such a way that I had to strain my neck to see any of this. I thought about the pain in my spine, and the ache in my jaw and in my head, and about how I needed a drink of water, badly.

Daddy was strapped to the oak board with leather belts and cable ties. They dragged him into the room and propped him up against the wall that had been left vacant. His hands and wrists were coated in blood and his arms were spattered with it. Blood covered his face too and there were great clots of it on his forehead. On his left side, his white cotton vest was drenched crimson. His feet were bare and bound and they were rubbed and bleeding also. Everywhere the blood was mixed with dirt and mud and leaves and grasses and tar and soil from the land about, and red moved to black-brown.

When he was brought in his eyes were closed. Slowly he opened them and fixed them on mine. He looked over at Cathy, whose attention was as captured. The men who had brought him were busy ensuring his bonds were tight. Others looked at his hands and arms and legs or about them or at each other. None but my sister and I looked at Daddy's eyes, a stark white, bright like two stars in a bloody firmament.

He groaned. He gurgled with each breath, liquid in his lungs.

Mr Price was the first to speak. 'It's a dark day, John. It's a dark day. And believe me, this brings me no pleasure.' He spoke quietly. 'But you know that I require justice. Our kind of justice. Make your confession and it will be quick. Relatively quick.'

Daddy said nothing. Perhaps he could not. His eyes moved from Mr Price, to me, to my sister, to Mr Price.

'You see that I brought your children here. I will be hard on them and you will see it,' said Price.

Still Daddy said nothing.

Mr Price nodded to the big man holding Cathy. She struggled as he pushed her down, pinned her to the floor and took a knife to her clothing. The garments shrieked and whined as he ripped them apart. His aim was not to pierce her skin but he nicked it as he made the incisions, and as she struggled, and as he cut and ripped. There was blood on her too now.

Yet she did not scream. Her mouth remained shut firm. Her eyes wide open.

A naked body is just a naked body. Shame is only in beholding. And if I looked at her without shame, she could stand before me naked without shame and there would be no power in it. For why should she care for the way these men, these inconsequential men, looked at her?

Her clothes were cut and her body was revealed. I looked at her with all the intensity I could muster. I looked into her eyes and caught them with mine and I tried with all my might to let her know. Know what? Something. That she was not alone. That these things were only as bad as you imagined them to be and that only she could steady her imagination. But when I looked I saw that she was there already. There, or perhaps elsewhere. A thin, durable film of miraculous unconcern had settled upon her. She was impervious.

She stood naked. The man was still holding her tight but he could hardly be seen behind her radiance. The cuts and spotting that had appeared on her near-translucent skin hardly held attention.

Daddy coughed. Some blood dribbled onto his thick black beard. It would need washing, I told myself. When this was done, Cathy and I would need to wash our father's clotted beard and matted hair. 'Please stop,' he whispered to Price.

Price stared back. 'Confess,' he said to Daddy.

Daddy opened his mouth to speak again. There was breath but none which had strength to catch his voice. He sighed, tried again, but again the air fell damp in his lungs.

'Mr Price,' said Cathy. Her voice was unusually soft but steady and cutting as the arc of an axe through air. 'I killed your son, Mr Price.'

Many in the room had been watching her. Many still watched her. But the mode of their gaze was so very different now it could hardly be given the same name.

Mr Price turned his head.

She said again, 'I killed your son, Mr Price.'

He smiled. Others followed suit. 'You tell me you had a hand in it? Lured him to the place, did you, so your father could rob him and kill him?'

Cathy shook her head. 'No,' she said. 'I did it alone. Daddy wandt there. He knew nothing about it. I was alone. I closed my hands around his neck and I squeezed. I squeezed and I squeezed and he struggled beneath me with all the strength he could muster but still I squeezed and he coundt do owt about it. And he just got weaker and weaker as I held his neck in my hands and he got bluer and bluer until he wandt breathing at all no more and still I held on just in case until my fingers ached. And then I let him go. And I covered him with that coat. And I dindt rob him, but that's by the by.'

Mr Price was stunned. His mouth gaped in incredulity. 'Get out of it,' he said. 'You dare. You dare lie to me, you little bitch. You dare.'

'It's not a lie. Why would I lie? Why would I lie now in this moment when you have us as captives here in this way? Why would I lie when I know truly that you will murder the person who saw to your son? And still I tell you, I killed him. I strangled him with these two little hands. And I'm not sorry. And I would do it again.'

Tom Price, the elder of the two brothers, had been leaning against the wall. He stepped forward. 'But how could you? You're a little girl?'

'She didn't,' interrupted Mr Price. 'Of course she didn't. She's playing with us. That's what they do.'

'I killed Charlie Price!' shouted Cathy. 'I killed Charlie Price!' she shouted again.

Charlie Price's father came forward himself this time. He raised his right hand behind his left ear and unfurled it on my sister's face with a loud crack.

The naked girl shut her eyes against the impact then opened them as quickly as if she had only turned and blinked and nothing more.

'I killed Charlie Price,' said Cathy again.

'Get her out of here,' said Mr Price to the room, to all of the other men who stood there, who had witnessed my sister's confession and had come to their own conclusions about the verity of her claims.

One of their number came forward after a moment of pause. He reached out a gloved hand and stroked her neck. 'I'll shut her up,' he stated blankly.

'Good,' replied Mr Price. 'Take her to the next room and do with her whatever you wish. And I mean whatever you wish. Make the most of her.'

The new man with the gloved hands took Cathy

from the grasp of the first and lifted her over his shoulder. She did not struggle. He removed her from the room and carried her into our hall then into a bedroom. I heard his footsteps. I heard the door click open and shut. I strained to hear more but there was nothing for several minutes.

In the meantime I was pulled up by my chin. It was Mr Price. The grip at my elbows was eased and I stood straight. Price asked, 'And what was your part in this, my boy? The man, the girl, and you,' he said. 'Your father, your sister, and you. Your sister admitted conspiracy. What of you?'

'Cathy dindt admit conspiracy,' I said. 'She told you that she did for your son and that she did for him alone.'

'Aye. And I don't believe her for one minute. A girl like that? Alone? No, I don't think so. I'm no fool.'

I said nothing.

Mr Price continued. 'I wonder,' he said, his voice more gentle than it had been. 'I wonder if you will come to resemble your mother or your father. In character, I mean. It is clear already that you have taken after your mother in physical appearance. But whose path will you follow? Will you end up like him?' He nodded towards Daddy, whose eyes had closed, whose breath had softened. 'Or will you end up like her?'

I lifted my head. I noticed creases in his golden skin and paler places at his lids. Shades of white-flecked pigeon-feather hair. Dry lips. Large ovaline nostrils flared when he inhaled. A flattish brow.

Perhaps he wanted me to ask. Perhaps he wanted for me to plead with him to tell me all about her. I cannot say that I did not want to know. I did. I had wanted to know all these years. I had wanted to ask it of Daddy, one time, on another day, on a very different type of day from this day, a day when we were here in this kitchen before these men came to stand here, any of the many days in the previous year when we had long hours to ourselves. We had had much to discuss but always had spoken little. Silence had been the mode of our exchanges. It had been the rule I had learnt.

So I remained silent, and the silence stayed my curiosity. My mother had come and gone. Until the last time when she had just gone. And not come.

When I was a very small boy I had sat in her arms as she rocked on a swing in the park behind Granny Morley's house. The chains that held the seat were rusted iron. They crackled as my mother leaned our weight against them, and ferrous crumbs dropped as she rocked. They hit the rubber beneath. I had held her tight. I had held on for dear life. But her fists crunched on those chains. She gripped them until her knuckles bleached out and until her palms were stained with that thin russet pigment, as if the metal had been treated and ground especially to colour that chalked skin precisely the shade of her very own vein-blood.

'She was always a grumpy girl,' said Mr Price. 'Always unhappy about something. You'd look at her and, likely as not, she'd have a downturned mouth and a frown on. What she had to be miserable about, God alone knows. Pretty face, of course, but she never made the most of it. I mean, I tried to do what I could for her. I would have married her if my boys' mother had died sooner. I made her a good offer. But she chose another path. She frittered her life away. Went about with the wrong sorts of people. Went to the wrong sorts of parties. The farm and the land she'd inherited all went to waste. And if there's one thing I hate, Daniel, it's waste. The waste of land especially. Good land, made barren. I can't stand it.'

Mr Price turned from me and went to the kitchen counter.

'So by the time I took her in, it was on very different terms. It had to be. She had disgraced herself. But I put a roof over her head, at least! Not that she ever showed any gratitude. And not that she stuck around. Your Daddy – if he is your Daddy – was working for me at the time, collecting rents, winning fights that I set up for him. And the two of them ran off together, didn't they. Ran off with a pile of cash, my wife's jewellery and a pair of 1960s Holland & Holland guns.'

He pulled at the brass ring handle of a drawer with a hooked, bloated thumb. It was the drawer that I had helped fit. I had not managed to fix the alignment quite right. It always stuck.

'Where she is now, God knows. Your Daddy couldn't hold her down for long either. Like I said, there was always that restless sadness about her. Always that inexplicable, unwarranted misery. If you told me she'd overdosed in a dark alley or Chapeltown brothel, I wouldn't be surprised.'

Daddy kept his knives in that drawer. Every Sunday evening he took them one by one from that drawer, sharpened them with a whetstone and returned them one by one in their particular arrangement.

Mr Price did not select the largest. That was a long, thin filleting knife with a gently curving edge. He chose instead a paring knife with a walnut handle and a stubbed, pointed blade roughly the length of my index finger.

He stepped towards Daddy. He stood close to him, such that they could inhale and exhale each other's breath. The air entered Daddy clean and left him with a bloody mist, and Mr Price breathed in that mist, the blood with it, and returned it dry.

Mr Price raised the blade and placed the point at

Daddy's shoulder. He struck through. The knife pierced the skin then went further. Mr Price had cut right through to the bone like he was jointing a stag. The blood gushed. Deep burgundy like thickened wine from deeper, more abundant vessels than the thin bright crimson blood splashed and smeared over his skin and candid white vest. The flow dribbled down his chest and arm both, soaked into his armpit.

Still Daddy's breath did not catch his voice box. He could not muster a scream. He sighed and looked upwards at the ceiling, though his face relaxed into a serene expression like he could see past it, up to the clouds and up to the stars. I did not know whether or not Daddy believed in heaven and hell. I did not think I had ever asked him. And if I had asked and been told, I had forgotten the answer.

Mr Price unplugged the knife. Another red spill.

'He'll bleed out,' Mr Price said to another man.

'Slowly,' said the other man, 'he's a big one. He may need another for good measure.'

'Oh I know it will be slow. And I'll put more on him before I'm done. But that one should be enough to do it.'

It was almost as if Mr Price was irritated by the advice, like he wanted to show that he knew what he was doing, like he, as much as any of the men here, could deal in matters of the body, in matters of slow death.

I watched Daddy as I had watched Cathy.

I wondered if he had come back for us and if that was why he had been found. I thought on what Vivien had said. And on what Ewart had intimated.

There was quiet from the other room. A silence that was unnerving. I cursed myself for being such a coward.

Then a whole lot of waiting. Mr Price leaned on the counter and he watched Daddy as he tried to keep his eyes open.

Then he came back and he stuck his blade into the softer place beneath Daddy's left kneecap. And then his right. Long, red socks. Price returned to the counter.

Tom's eyes were wide open now. It seemed as if he could not blink at all. Everything about his countenance was dry, parched, and guarded. His eyes were open wide but his mouth was shut tight. His lips were white: the outermost, cell-thin layer of skin had died and crumbled while we had been standing here. If he smiled the dead skin would crack. If he licked his lips, the dead skin would form a pallid, sticky paste.

Blood was pooling on the floor at Daddy's feet.

The door swung open.

My sister cast a long shadow. It was heavy, the colour of charcoal, the kind of shadow that can only be cast by fire. It flickered and spat. Its source, held in Cathy's left hand, had been hidden behind the door frame. She pulled it into view: a rag, doused in oil, tied around a bed post that she had pulled clean off its frame. Looped over her wrist was the wire handle of a tin bucket that swung dully as she moved her arm. It was filled with oil, and but a precarious two feet from the flaming torch.

In her right hand she held a shotgun, its butt locked to her side by her elbow, two thin fingers resting on its trigger.

Her hands and arms were coated with a thick layer of blood. Not her own. It was deepest red at her thumbs and fingertips, and lightest and brightest as it moved up her forearms.

It was as if she had plunged her limbs deep into that man's guts.

I imagined him stretched out on the bed exhibiting a rough, gaping, bloody hole.

I could not imagine how she had done it.

She stepped into the room. She was still naked. She had found the bucket, the oil, the shotgun. She had not stopped to clothe herself.

And she shone. She had poured oil onto her own skin, and over her head onto her face and her thick, now slicked, black hair.

The man holding me loosened his grip. He recoiled like a spider from the light. I took my chance and leapt to the other side of the room, away from Mr

Price, his surviving son, and his men. I took a place between Daddy, bloody, pinned to the oak board, and Cathy, her back as straight as the two barrels she pointed at Mr Price's breast.

The scene had changed: the tempo, the climate, the aspect. The presence of the flickering flame shifted the saturation. Reds were now hot. Blues became muddy. Whites took on a tempered orange sheen. The skin of men's faces, pulled back in dismay, tarnished and bruised in the new shadows. The slate tiles rippled between matte and satin like a frozen-thawed-refrozen layer of black ice.

'One of you will untie my father,' she said, simply.

There was silence. Nobody moved.

'She doesn't have the first idea how to use one of those,' said a squat, bald man who had not spoken before.

Cathy shot him.

At that range the shrapnel had little time to spray. The full cartridge tore through his stomach and took out a cupboard door behind. The man dropped to the ground and shook a violent shake.

Her aim was natural. I expected no less.

Tom's jeans darkened at his crotch as his piss spread. One of the men rattled the handle of the back door. It was locked. Cathy shot him. He too crumpled on the floor.

'Stop!' shouted Mr Price. 'Tony, do as she asks.'

Tony was a tall man with faded tattoos the length of his long torso. He took the knife from his employer's hand. He used it to cut through Daddy's bonds, beginning at his ankles, then moving to his wrists. It was slow work. The knots were tight and the ropes were tough.

Free, Daddy fell away from the table top and shrunk against the back wall. Blood rubbed against the paintwork and soaked through to the plaster. Tony returned to his master's side.

'He's already dead, Cathy,' said Mr Price. 'He'll bleed out. There's no helping him.'

'I can see that.'

The torch was burning lower, closer to the bucket of oil.

The crowd quaked. Men shifted uneasily, dancing on the spot with a desire to run but with no chosen nor possible direction.

Keeping her eyes on Mr Price at all times, Cathy said quietly, only to me, 'It's your time to leave.'

I glanced at Daddy. He was fading fast, slipping between states.

I saw the door behind my sister, open, and from there just a few steps to the front door, then the outside.

I remembered what she had said to me earlier that evening. I remembered my promise.

In a single, smooth motion Cathy flung both

bucket and torch into the air on a trajectory towards Mr Price.

As flame and oil converged at the height of their arc I slipped through the open door and threw myself out of the house into the cool evening air. Fire erupted behind me. I could hear it and feel it. I could see its luminous contours on the damp grass at my feet.

I ran. I ran and I ran. I ran through the night and noted nothing that I saw. Not the pools of water lying about the land, nor the dark storm clouds in the sky, nor the droplets of rain shooting sharp and fast, spitting at me then dripping down my face.

I ran as quickly as I could, as quickly as I had ever run before, through this landscape that I knew but did not in this moment see. I might have run for hours. I ran until I fell.

Chapter Twenty-Two

Smoke moved over the water. The shadows were long, thin teeth, and light curled around the trees, between trunks and crooked, clad branches. It made parchment of the leaves. It made dust of the morning dew. The water below shone brighter than the sky above and it illuminated the smoke from beneath like a vivid moon behind papyrus clouds.

There was murky water on my tongue. It flowed into my cheeks and out again and the taste of wet then drying earth lingered with each flushed mouthful. The pool padded against the left side of my face and entered my nostrils and eased down my throat. I sipped on dirt and tasted iron blood.

The fire had been built of many parts. It had been built of gas and light and sparks, of flames and ripples and currents. It had devoured damp air and sapless wood and engulfed a small pocket of the cool night. I had run a long way. I had stopped here and settled. I had stooped for water, any water I could find, and raised it to my lips with two cupped hands, trembling, and I had lain my head on the shore for a while, just for a while, and I had slept, it seems, and woken, before I had noted the place.

I could still smell the fire though I was far away. Resin from the burnt embers stuck at the back of my throat, from the rafters of the roof and the ash floorboards. And the sight of it, too, was stuck some-where at the back of my head, behind my eyes, the sight of those curling, forked tongues licking familiar figures. And the sound of it still thick in my ears: a hiss, a groan, a beat, as beams bent and broke. My skull was full.

The smoke was mist, not smoke at all. It rose from the reservoir in the morning calor. The reservoir was five miles from the copse, perhaps nearer on a direct path, over hedges, ditches and planted fields. That was the route I had taken, I think. My course had been as straight as a train track. I had not swayed from side to side one bit, I think, though my steps had undulated as I had jumped over banks then down to the boggy parts to trudge through acrid organic tar, the aggregate sludge of every autumn rotting. Either the night had been caught with haze or it had been my memory that had reduced solid shapes to spectres. All was unknown, I recall, though I had trodden those tracks many times before. But the levels look different after dark, and the world is distinct for each individual, and I had been made new as I had walked and I had seen the land like it had been new too.

I must have slept again: my eyes were shut. I must have slept without stirring despite the brightening horizon. I slept until I felt another wetness on my cheeks. Damp bristles moved over my brow and caught on my eyelids. A new smell met the igneous residue. A musk. And lips. These were lips. Coarse, meaty, jagged lips, but kind, somehow inviting. And teeth that knocked at my scalp as the lips drew in lumps of my hair. And a tongue – long, viscous – moved down to my neck and wrapped itself around my jaw.

I opened my eyes. The head of a horse. Two large brown eyes, like snooker balls, rolled to scan my face, then the world around, then my face. The horse snorted and tossed her sooty forelock. The sun was full in the sky now, though not high, and as the horse swayed, her head moved in front of it, making a dark silhouette of her otherwise rusty fur, and a stilted halo around her otherwise silky mane.

'Who are you?'

It was a question to the horse. In my state of half dream, it was a necessary question.

The horse continued to ruffle my hair. Her rider answered, 'It's Vivien, Daniel. It's Vivien.'

If relief were a thing it was possible to feel when the full gush of dread was still swilling within, casked and stoppered, then I might have felt relief. But as it was, the sight of this friend, without much reason, put fear to boil. She did not dismount.

'There's been a fire,' she said.

'Yes.'

'A fire at your house.'

'Yes,' I said. 'I was there. I ran away.'

'I had hoped . . .'

'How did you find me?'

'I've been riding for two hours,' she replied. 'You look ill.'

'Not ill,' I said.

Vivien rearranged the reins in her gloved hands. The horse stepped to one side and planted four hooves such that she stood side on, and Vivien turned too to look upon me. I raised myself up out of the dirt with the palms of my hands, then stood up.

'Have you found anyone else?' I knew that nobody had made it out, save for me.

'I saw a figure.'

'Who?'

'I saw the fire last night, all the way from my house. At first I thought it was a bonfire and wondered why I hadn't been told so that I could come up. And then I saw that it was too big. Far too big to be a bonfire. And I put on my coat and left the house and began to walk up the track. The wind was blowing in my face, so the smoke was too. Directly at me. For a while I stopped being able to see the flames, the smoke was so thick. But then I got closer, as close as I could get against heat, and saw your house. It was on fire. And I saw you, what I thought to be you, rushing down the hill away from me, running as fast as you could. I would have followed but, somehow, I couldn't. I remained. I watched the blaze, I watched as the house fell apart. I thought I saw figures inside, but I couldn't be sure. I couldn't see well enough. I think the smoke had scorched my eyes, I don't know. I don't know if that's possible. And when it was almost over, such a long time later, I thought I saw a figure emerge. But it couldn't have been. But I thought I saw a thin figure emerge. As the dawn was coming up.'

'Who?'

'I couldn't say,' she said. 'I don't know if it was real.'

'Could it have been my sister?'

'I don't know. I don't really know what I saw. I just had the image, and now just the memory of the image.'

'But it could have been.'

'Possibly.' She peered down at me but I could not seem to hold her gaze. I looked out towards the reservoir.

'Why did I run?' I asked.

'Running was the only thing to do.'

'I left them.'

'It was the only thing to do, Daniel.'

'Cathy told me to.'

'She was right to.'

The reservoir appeared to lilt from side to side. I stared instead at a sickening ash tree on its far bank. It was too brittle to sway with the wind.

After a while, she said: 'You could come home with me.'

This time I looked up at her. It was a kind offer. 'Thank you, but I have got my own family.'

We stood for a moment: Vivien, the horse, and a lanky lad, barely fifteen.

'Which way did she go?'

'Daniel, I don't know. The figure I thought I saw, I thought it moved towards the tracks. I ran soon after, back to mine to get Daisy, to come and find you. I saw nothing clearly.'

'Towards the tracks?'

'Yes?'

'Then where?'

'I didn't see.'

I nodded. I looked about me, to see if I had left anything on the ground. There was nothing, just an indentation where I had lain. I had brought nothing with me. I had nothing to bring. For no reason at all, I scuffed the marks in the sand with my foot. I would leave no trace, no tracks. No hunter would find me.

'I'll be going then,' I said to Vivien, and, in part, to Daisy.

Daisy blinked feather lashes. Vivien let out an agitated sigh.

'Remember what I said, Daniel.'

I walked away from the reservoir, and away from the woman and her horse, following approximately the route I must have taken the night before.

Needless to say, the idea of returning to our house on the hill was suffocating. I watched my feet take each step, one then another. Their tilt, the way they slapped the earth, the way the toes bent.

I did not look back, though a couple of times I heard the horse's hooves stamp and drag, as Vivien kept there to watch me go.

After around half a mile, I came to a wooden, slatted bridge, barely more than four planks thrust together and stitched with rusted, hooked nails that led across a thin dike. The furrow carried excess water after heavy rain. These parts flooded regularly. In winter, and after summer storms, great torrents rushed from the nearby hills to the flat lands.

There had been rain last night, I remembered. It had rained as I had walked, though I had hardly noticed. It had been all around. I remembered suddenly: fattened, matured plugs of rain had cascaded past me and bounced at my feet. A summer storm. I had walked in it then slept in it. My clothes were still damp. And the reservoir had been high, too. High enough to slap my face, though I had rested on an upper bank.

I quickened my pace. I had to run. The whole landscape was wet.

The figure Vivien had seen. There was more than a chance it was Cathy, saved miraculously from the fire by storm to walk through the smoke to the only remaining landmark she could find in the gloom: the railway track.

I ran and ran. A cloud of smoke, soot and heavy steam rested on the hill. It filled the void where the house had been. I was thankful that I was spared the sight of the absence where, for a blissful year, there had been a home.

As I got closer, I saw baked ribs, the empty structure's blackened frame. I saw cinders that stood precariously from the ground to the branches of charred trees, burning wood on a scale I had never witnessed. I saw a kind of black that was new to me, condensed, compacted, opaque.

I walked on. I had no desire to inspect the remains:

there was no telling what I would find. Besides, the railway track, and the possibility of my sister, lay ahead. But as I walked on past the burnt house, past the burnt chicken coop, past the slim charred vegetable patch, past the ashen copse, I was harried by glinting sparks, the biting revenants of a shredded inferno. They swept and swirled about me like gulls at a trawler. I was their last scrap, their last taste of living tissue and hope of supper before they fell like those before them to the damp earth. I walked on, and they fell.

I came to the tracks. Two sets. Four cords of iron, running as straight as rainwater falls, from north to south. Iron stretched between magnetic poles. The wooden sleepers were dark with damp. The stone ballast was slick. I climbed the embankment, though the grass was slippery, and stood upon the cess. I looked to my left and I looked to my right. I saw no one. But if Cathy had fled the house and come to the tracks she would have continued, and she could be a long way off by now. I looked left and I looked right. North to Edinburgh or south to London. I made my choice and walked.

VI

The man drives off in his jittering hulk and I do not think on him again. I am waiting for someone.

I wait out by the station. Not the building itself but the web of tracks that bring passengers and freight to this city from every point of the compass. I watch people come and go and see that there are others like me sitting out by the tracks and sleeping in the undergrowth and in outhouses and sheds. I build small fires and cook what food I find and catch.

But I know that my time here is temporary. I am waiting for someone.

When I am not waiting I roam the city. The stone here is darker. The buildings are built from rock hued from a different quarry. I had not known that towns and cities had their own characters. For me there was only ever blanched limestone and red brick. From a distance I see tall women with dark hair and I follow them until I am close enough to see their faces and discern that they are not her. This is how I pass my time.

Some of the people out by the tracks speak to me and ask questions. The curiosity of strangers.

Midges dance among horseflies among thrips. They coalesce to a swirling throng and circle an invisible centre like electrons around a nucleus. A lone bee surfs beneath them and pauses from its journey to be shaded by docks. Pale moths hang loosely in the haze, their wings luminous, then dim, then luminous, as they beat against an inevitable descent.

Acknowledgements

Thank you to all those at Artellus Ltd., and particularly to Leslie Gardner and Darryl Samaraweera. Thank you to Becky Walsh for her patience, meticulousness and risk-taking, and for seeing the potential in my early manuscript. Thank you to the rest of the team at John Murray, including Tom Duxbury, and especially to Yassine Belkacemi, for his enthusiasm for the project.

Thank you to my early readers: Alastair Bealby, Sophie Howard, Carla Suthren and Lisa Girdwood.

Thanks and love to Caroline Mozley, Harold Mozley, Olivia Mozley and Neil Johnson.

Thank you most of all to Megan Girdwood, without whom I could never have finished this novel, let alone had the courage to seek its publication.